Hazel Rye

Also by Vera and Bill Cleaver

DELPHA GREEN & COMPANY

DUST OF THE EARTH

ELLEN GRAE

GROVER

I WOULD RATHER BE A TURNIP

THE KISSIMMEE KID

LADY ELLEN GRAE

A LITTLE DESTINY

ME TOO

THE MIMOSA TREE

THE MOCK REVOLT

QUEEN OF HEARTS

TRIAL VALLEY

WHERE THE LILIES BLOOM

THE WHYS AND WHEREFORES OF
LITTABELLE LEE

Hazel Rye

VERA and BILL CLEAVER

J. B. LIPPINCOTT New York

HAZEL RYE

 Printed in the United States of America. For information address J. B. Lippincott Junior Books, 10 East 53rd Street, New York, N.Y. 10022. Published simultaneously in Canada by Fitzherry & Whiteside Limited, Toronto.

Designed by Joyce Hopkins
1 2 3 4 5 6 7 8 9 10
First Edition

Library of Congress Cataloging in Publication Data

Cleaver, Vera.
Hazel Rye.

SUMMARY: An eleven-year-old girl, with no appreciation for land and growing things, finds her values beginning to change when she agrees to let an impoverished family live in a small house she owns, in exchange for working in the surrounding orange grove.

[1. Orange—Fiction] I. Cleaver, Bill.
II. Title.
PZ7.C57926Haz 1983 [Fic] 81-48603
ISBN 0-397-31951-7 AACR2
ISBN 0-397-31952-5 (lib. bdg.)

Hazel Rye

1

Seated on the front porch of the Rye home, Hazel and her father were occupied, he with the comics section of the Sunday paper and she with two textbooks, dividing her wrathful attention between them. The books' pages were black with numbers and words, and presently she slammed both volumes shut and sat forward and with a thrust in her voice said, "Too many how-many's. That's why they retained me and I have to take sixth grade over when school starts again. Too many how-many's. Teacher always wants to know if I take so many of this and multiply it by so many of that how many I'll have, and if I don't spit out the right answer, she gets purple in the face. She gets purpler when I tell her I didn't read and didn't write what she told me to read and write. She knows I didn't. She knows I hate words. I wonder who invented them."

"Somebody who wanted to aggravate us, I guess," said Millard Rye. "But if I was you I'd forget them books for a while and think about something else. School's out now. Think about us. Think about play. I'll tell you something about me that I never told you before. School was always kind of loopsey-loosey to me too. I had me a teacher who always made me feel guilty as a dog at a icebox when I didn't know the answers, and I never did and it hasn't ever hurt me any."

With her foot Hazel pushed the books to the porch railing. "I'm fascinating," she said.

"What?" said her father.

"Fascinating. That's what my teacher told me. She wanted to know what I thought I was going to do with my life. I told her when I got old enough, I was going to quit school and go to driving a taxi and make three hundred dollars a week. That's how much Donnie made last week. Did he tell you?"

"Your brother don't take time out to tell me anything since him and Vannie Lee got married," replied Millard Rye. "I stopped by their house yesterday on my way home from work, but wasn't anybody home."

"They've got a new car," said Hazel. "Black and orange. The orange part makes it look like it's on fire except there's no smoke." Grandly indifferent, empty of mind, she lay back in her chair. During the week the weather had come gunning for Florida's Ridge, that central inland section of the state occupied by springs and lakes and low, hump-shouldered limestone hills. But now the Sabbath was come and the sky was meek, without sound.

Showing new green-sprout growth beneath the crowns of dead branches, dead from the past winter's freeze, some of the trees in the old citrus grove adjoining the Rye property hailed the early June sun. Others, more severely injured by cold damage, still slept their gray, bare sleep.

The three acres of trees and the four-room cabin standing forsaken in the deadest part of the grove were Hazel's, a wheedling gift presented to her by her father during one of her silent-treatment arguments with him. After four days of her sulking, he hadn't given in on the question of allowing her to have her ears pierced, but had come wooing her with his peace offering. Smiling his sympathy and yet his authority, he showed her the childishly drawn document that he said transferred ownership of the grove from him to her.

Holding fast to her anger and glaring her contempt, Hazel said, "I don't want it."

Her father had met her glare with one of his own. "You better not turn it down so quick. The trees are slouches, but the land is still there and it's a good investment. Someday when I'm gone and you're out of ready cash, you can sell it for a lot more than I paid for it."

"When you're gone?" said Hazel. "Where are you going?"

"That's not clear to me," answered her father. "And that's not what I'm talking about. I'm talking about I might not always be here to take care of you, so you'd better take me up on this offer. Not many little daughters can say they own three acres and a house to boot. You better think about this now."

"I already have," said Hazel. "I don't like those old corpses over there, and I don't like you either."

This last wasn't so. She adored her father, and

after two more days of sulking, she accepted his gift on the condition that she be allowed to do with it as she pleased. It pleased her to do nothing with the grove and the house in it. At school she told her teachers and classmates that she had become a property owner, but this news was doubted and did nothing to forward her popularity. She waited two weeks before offering to sell the gift back to her father for twenty-five dollars, but he only hugged her and laughed.

She called her father Millard because that was his first name, and though her mother did not think this was the least bit cute or funny, she kept her disapproval to herself, for Millard Rye was a good husband and provider, didn't cuss or drink or smoke, ate what was placed in front of him with little or no complaint, and didn't snore or grind his teeth in his sleep. He was a carpenter of good reputation who usually employed one or two helpers, and every morning he rose and cooked his own breakfast and Hazel's. All of his days except Sundays were spent at heavy labor. At reading and writing he was backward, yet his spoken language was colorful. He had a father and an older, unmarried sister living in Missouri, but the years went by and went by, with only cards at Christmas to remind. Millard

Rye said that he and his sister weren't anything alike. It gave him pleasure to look at the younger of his two children and see a physical and mental extension of himself.

To Hazel on this country morning, life was whole and appropriate except for her unpierced ears and the hated textbooks. She was eleven and was not plagued by either talent or ambition. Her short, sturdy legs supported her short, compact body, her head sported a thick growth of short, brown hair, her almond-colored eyes looked out at the world and asked of it a stern question: "So what?"

The world did not say.

What the white ibis on its way to a marsh roost called out as it sailed over the Rye house had never caused Hazel to look up, to pause and listen. She had never gazed at a tree and wondered about its parents or personality. She had never held a seed in her hand and thought about its past or its future. Her father thought that she fell into the category of perfection. This was not an opinion shared by her mother, who was homely as a cucumber and possessed of a nervous, slipshod nature.

The mother's name was Ona, and to her the keeping of the Rye home was an accomplishment worse than none, a notion in which Hazel believed also.

So it was that on this placid morning, conditions with the Ryes were no more astir, were no different, than on any other Sunday. Their kitchen and other rooms were in need of care. In her bedroom Ona Rye slept, and on the porch Millard Rye discarded one comics sheet and took up another. Having nothing else to occupy her eyesight, Hazel watched her father. In the town of Echo Spring, eight miles north of the Ryes' entrance gate, church bells pealed, calling the faithful to worship. The Ryes did not seek what the bells meant. They did not take God personally. In their setting God was neither beautiful or hideous. He was featureless, without life.

To the Rye setting on this important day came the family of Poole. Hazel watched as their car drew to a halt at the Rye gate. Attached to the car's rear bumper by means of a wooden tongue was a small two-wheeled hauling trailer. It was plainly homemade and plainly loaded. Tacked to its four corner posts was a square piece of protecting canvas. The rear seat of the car was packed with two children and what obviously were housekeeping properties. The front seat contained a woman driver and one more passenger. The woman spoke a command before they all stepped out, and in the manner of the poor but honest came up the walkway to the steps of the porch.

With the look of a guarding mastiff, Hazel leaned forward, examining the woman, the teen-aged girl, and the two younger children. She judged the boy, who had a backpack strapped to his shoulders, to be her own age or slightly older. She thought he was one of those persons who always had to be busy as a cat on a tin roof, one who would grub away at any and every kind of hackwork till he either dropped or was told it was time to quit. The older girl looked as if she had chewed on and swallowed every problem there was and if she hadn't solved them all yet she soon would. The younger girl had cocker-spaniel eyes. She had never hated anything and never would. To Hazel, the woman appeared as one of those pioneer ladies seen in Western movies, the type that not only drives the mules westward-ho but gets out and helps them pull the wagon.

It was to the woman that Hazel spoke. "If you're looking for Echo Spring it's up the road about eight miles, and if you want water you can go around to the back and help yourselves. Use the can by the spigot. That's what we always let strangers drink out of."

The woman said, "Well, thank you." And alone climbed the porch steps and stood before Millard Rye. She said, "Hey. Could I have a word with you?"

"Hey, yourself," responded Millard Rye from behind his comics sheet. "If you're here to collect your husband's pay from last week, I hope you brought me a note from him telling me you could. The last time I paid off a wife with no say-so from the husband, she lied about it, so I had to shuck out twice."

"My husband doesn't work for you and never did," said the woman. "He was a grove caretaker and died six months ago while trying to help put out a brush fire."

Still hiding behind his paper, Millard Rye said, "Dying is something nobody should have to put up with. It don't make sense for people to be put here and strain themselves from the time they grow their first teeth till their last ones either fall out or have to be yanked out, just so they can die. These-here funny papers make more sense. Had it been me arranging things, I'd have done a better job."

"Would you," said the uninvited guest. She had red wrists and a goose neck and looked like somebody who could whet an axe and use it. "It's hard for me to try to talk with you with that paper between us."

Hazel's father lowered his comics sheet, and the look he gave the pioneer woman rebuked her very presence. "Sundays," he said, "is the only days I get to look at my paper and I have to go clear into town after it. What can I do for you?"

"I told her the water was out back and she and her kids could use the can to drink out of," said Hazel, "but she wants something else." And as if the intruder had lost the ability to both speak and understand the English language, added, "Maybe she's hungry. You want me to give her what's left of the ham we had last night? You said it was too salty because Mama didn't cook it right. We're just going to throw it out anyway."

"We stopped," said the wagon lady, the whetter of axes, "because we're looking for a house in the country to rent. Earlier this morning we drove by here and saw that the little one in your grove is vacant. If you would consider renting it to us, I promise we'd take good care of it. I know that right at the moment we can't look like much to you, but we're honorable. I'm Josephine Poole. People who know me call me Jo, and my boy there is Felder and the little girl is Jewel and the big one is Wanda. What do you think a fair rental price for your little house would be?"

To avoid the woman's granite gaze, Millard Rye slid his eyes past her shoulder to the three standing silent and still in the yard. "Missus, you don't want to live in that house. Most of it is full of tools all rusted, and besides, that's where my little girl and I go of an evening when we want to look at something special on television or fry us some fish. My wife can't stand television and the smell of fish makes her sick. I forgot to tell you, that house belongs to my little girl here and she don't want to rent it."

"That's right," said Hazel. "I don't want to rent it. As soon as it gets winter again and some northerners come down, I'm going to sell it to one of them."

"Felder is only twelve but he's good with tools," said Jo Poole. "In the summers when he wasn't in school, he used to work with his father. If you rented us the house, we'd clear all of the tools out of it. Possibly Felder could clean them up. You could sell them."

"No," said Millard Rye. "See, we're private people and we like our privacy."

"We wouldn't disturb your privacy," urged Jo. "We're private people too. Most of the time you wouldn't even know we were here. Felder and Jewel always have things to do and Wanda and I will be gone most of the day. We'll be working."

"At what?"

"Anything we can find. There are jobs in town. Of course, Wanda won't work when school commences again, but you won't ever have to fret about your rent. I'll always have it."

"How old," inquired Hazel's father, "is Wanda?"

"Sixteen."

"I got a boy eighteen year old and he quit when he was sixteen. Smart. Takes home three hundred dollars a week."

"Wanda is going to finish high school," said Jo. "After that she intends to go on to higher learning. She wants to get into law."

"That's fine," said Millard Rye. "That's fine, but we still don't want to rent you our house."

"Maybe," said Hazel. "I wouldn't mind renting it to you for just a month. But I'd want my money right away. Could you pay me now?"

"No," said Hazel's father, "she can't pay you

now. She hasn't got any money. Be quiet and let me handle this."

"It's my house," sniffed Hazel.

Her father addressed himself to Jo Poole. "Missus, I can see you're in a predicament. I recognize it because I've been in some myself, but I'm a frank man so I'll tell you frankly, about all I can do for you is hand you a few dollars to help you get on down the road a ways, and if you want the ham, you'd be welcome to that, but I can't go no farther than that."

Masking her disappointment with courtesy, Jo Poole turned and looked toward the grove. A dingy mist occupied its darkest places, and the wind blew whispering through its tallest weeds. Said Jo, "Well, you're kind, but we couldn't take anything from you unless you'd let us do a little work for you. I think we can afford that much pride. We have some foodstuffs with us and we're not above sleeping in the car."

"Oh, look here," responded Hazel's father with an irritated rasp in his voice. "Why don't you just take the ham and the dollars and go on? If it was me, that's what I'd do. You won't ever see us again, so what would be the difference? I help people out a little all the time and most of them don't hit a lick for it. For instance I give to the Salvation Army every Christmas and all they do is ring their bells and say thank you."

The child Jewel had come to the steps and was staring at Hazel's father. "One time," she said, "after my daddy died, we got to eat at the Salvation Army's house and they let us sleep there too." Travel stained as were the other Pooles and with a desperate humility, she said, "We don't have any bells to ring, but if you'd let us do some work for you, Mama would take the ham and the money and then we'd go."

"Oh, good grief a-mercy," snorted Millard Rye and gave his attention to Hazel. "Lady, go find these people some work to do and let's get through with this."

"Work," said Hazel, an observer of work, and looked around as if she might see a pile of it emerge, quaking and staggering, from the house. Smudged with soil and handprints, its glass entrance door stood open. In its wide, grooved sill, a dead roach lay on its back. "We don't have any work," said Hazel. "It's all done. Mama and I did everything yesterday except the kitchen." She wanted the Pooles to go, for they were not, in her view, civilized. They all looked like they belonged to the woods, to leaping fires and boiling rivers. From television and town movies Hazel had learned all about such, and it wouldn't have surprised her a bit to see Wanda whip out a jar of bear grease and smear her hair with its contents. Or to see Felder reach into his pocket, draw a musket from it, and empty its balls or powder or whatever it was in muskets that killed people, first into her father's belly and then her own. Yet caught up in the Pooles' problem and aware of her role as daughter of the house, Hazel strolled ahead of them through the house to the kitchen.

At sight of this room so shamed, so knuckled under, Jo Poole put a hand to her forehead and said, "My land."

Shrewishly Hazel said, "Well, I told you, Mama and I didn't do this room yesterday and you said you wanted to work, but if it scares you, you can go on. We don't need you."

Jo was not offended. Her response was light and fresh, as to a light, fresh wind blowing through the fouled room. "Possibly not, but this kitchen does. Where is your mama, honey?"

"Asleep," answered Hazel. "And don't any of you wake her up to ask her anything. She takes a lot of sleep because she's very nervous. If you need anything, you ask me where it is and I'll tell you."

Already at feud with the sink, which was overloaded with soiled dishes, Wanda fished a brown rag from its sodden depths and, after observing it for a second, made a ball of it and plopped it into an open, pasteboard box containing emptied jars, cans, a ham rind, and other kitchen wastes. With her foot she gave the box a shove, and as it moved past Felder to a new resting place, he gave it a moment of serious attention and offered a positive opinion. "What this room needs is a shovel."

"We'll need some clean rags," said Jo glancing at Hazel. "Do you have any? And what's your name, dear?"

"There are some rags under the sink," said Hazel, "and my name is Hazel."

Wanda issued an order to Felder. "Take this box out and dump it in the garbage." Preparing to properly wash them, she was transferring the dishes from the sink to the stove top. "Whew," she said. "Whew."

"The garbage people won't come out from town to get ours so we have to bury it," said Hazel, light flaring in her eyes. Her sentiment for the Pooles was not pity, nor yet much curiosity, but resentment, for they were spoiling her Sunday. The way the boy Felder thumbed his chin, and whatever it was that dwelled in his face, made her think of her teacher, a woman whose blood pumped poetry, who sat mooning out the window during study periods as if she could see something out there nobody else could see.

Felder was like that. He had gone to the door that opened out onto the back porch and was standing there looking out toward the grove, as though he could see something in its ruin that persons with ordinary eyes would never suspect was there.

"The box," said Hazel bluntly, upholding command of the situation. "It's not going to walk out of here by itself, so you'll have to carry it. You can leave your backpack here. Nobody will steal it. What's in it?"

"Things," said Felder. He tightened the straps to the pack, securing it to his shoulders, and came back for the box, hefting it.

"Dad doesn't want any more holes dug around the house, so we'll have to take the garbage to the grove and bury it," said Hazel. "There's a shovel in the grove house and you can use that. I'll show you where to dig the hole. I don't want it dug just any old place, because when my friends come to my parties, we always play games in the grove in certain places." In this last statement there was not a syllable of truth. The truth was she had never given a party in the grove or anywhere else for her friends, for she had none; and further to the truth, she did not give a rap about where in the grove the new hole might be dug, nor for the grove itself, so slouchy, so sick, dying yet refusing to die. Like the old people who sat on the sidewalk benches in Echo Spring, passing their empty days with their empty mouths hanging open. One of these bench sitters claimed to be ninety-five years old and always shared his ice-cream cone with a companion, a disgusting sight.

Even when owned by another, an elderly lady who came once a year to look at it from the window of her car, the grove had always been a scene of neglect. But in spite of this, the grove was still passable in Hazel's eyes. It was in the deepest months of winter, when wind lashed the Ridge and the trees would groan and creak as if in the grip of some great torment, that Hazel disliked them most. She thought all of the commotion was unnecessary, and a dream to sell the place was her favorite mental entertainment. With the money she received for it she meant to go to a doctor in town, a young one who could see good, and have her ears pierced.

With or without her father's permission she meant to do this. After that she would go to Price's jewelry store and buy a pair of pure-gold earrings. If there was any money left over she would buy a car. It would be purple and shaped like a rocket. Until she was old enough to do so herself, she would hire somebody to drive it, to take her places.

Meanwhile here it was, the grove, sighing its life away, feeding the bugs, drinking the rain when it came, sucking from the earth whatever food its roots could find. Most all of it useless as a raincoat to a whale.

And meanwhile here was this immediate, this Felder Poole with his pack of things and the box of garbage, jogging ahead of her through the backyard, through the gate and into the grove, correcting his path every now and then to peer and peer as though the trees and the dry, drained soil around them were his very business in life. Out beyond the grove lay an area of high pineland, and mixed with the pines were stands of blackjack oaks and live oaks.

The sky was tender blue, and Felder, stealing time from his chore, set the box on the ground and hunched down beside it. He was all eyes. His eyes were candid and level and they coveted. Coveted the creaky little house and pioneer citrus trees surrounding it, coveted the wide air, coveted everything.

Uncertain of just what it was she was witnessing, Hazel said, "Well, it isn't all that much."

"No," said Felder. "Not now it isn't. But it's more than you think."

"How do you know what I think?"

"I've seen other girls like you."

"Like me? You've seen other girls like me? Where?"

"Everywhere."

"You've been everywhere?"

"No, not everywhere, but to a few places."

"What for?"

Felder's look was clean. "To see. My dad wanted us to see the places we read about in our books, so when he had time and we had the money, we went and looked."

"And where you went, you saw some girls that looked like me?"

"Some did and some didn't. I never pay much mind to how girls look. It's how they are that counts."

"And how do you think I am?"

"Average."

With sharp displeasure Hazel drew in her breath. "I own this grove and I own that house over there. My dad gave it all to me. Is that average?"

"My dad," said Felder, "didn't leave me much. Just the whole world, so I'd have a place where I could make my living."

"And next winter when the people from the north come back again, I'm going to sell it all and then I'll be rich," said Hazel.

Felder's calm study offered its doubt.

"Rich," insisted Hazel. "You know what rich is, don't you?"

"We haven't had too much to do with each other," said Felder. "My dad always told me if I wanted to get rich, I'd have to look to the ends of my sleeves for help."

"To the ends of your sleeves," said Hazel. "What's that mean?"

"Hands," said Felder. "Usually people have hands at the ends of their sleeves, and a lot of them do work with them, and some get rich. I don't know much about rich, but I guess I know it when I see it and I don't see it here. Since the freeze last winter there are too many little groves all up and down the Ridge like this one, so even Yankees who don't know citrus trees from telephone poles know better than to pay much for them. I don't see how you figure on getting rich on what's here. Now, if you'd doctor your trees and make them well again so they'd grow oranges again, that'd be different."

"I don't want to have to doctor these trees," said Hazel with all the detachment of the safe and the safely reared. "Besides, I don't know how."

Felder had grace and he was manly. "Well," he said, "it's no job for a girl like you. It's for people like me. I started learning how to doctor trees when I was eight. You want me to bury the garbage here? I'll run to the house for the shovel if you want me to. You wait here and make up your mind while I'm gone. Where should I look for the shovel?"

"I think it's under one of the beds or in the bathroom," replied Hazel. "You might have to look for it, but you don't need to run. Leave your backpack here. It'll be safe with me." She watched as Felder divested himself of the pack and lowered it to the ground.

Near at hand in the arm of a tree, a feathered singer spun out tart notes, and Hazel, after eyeing the backpack for a moment, drew it toward her and knelt beside it. Its buckled straps were a slight nuisance, its lock was broken and opened to her touch. Unaware that she was adding a new dimension to her own, Hazel gazed upon the whole of Felder's life, his wonderworld.

There were jars of seeds and pods, two books whose titles stated that they were about citrus growing, a plastic bag containing round, pencil-sized twigs tucked into wads of moist, spongy plant material. There was a banded swatch of transparent tapes, a sharp knife, and in yet another plastic bag there was a large ball unlike any she had seen. It looked soft as living flesh looks soft, and it drew and held her attention. With both hands she reached into the pack and withdrew the bag in which the ball was contained. It lay as though dead, yet something in the vital feel of it quickened her curiosity.

She reached for the knife and, setting the ball on the ground, cut into it, making a small wound; and as though something in it lived, it sighed and spit a plume of gray-green dust.

"Alive," whispered Hazel. "Oh, you're alive." Shocked and strangely disturbed and excited, half expecting to see the spiral of dust followed by a spout of blood, she waited for the ball's tiny scream, for some sound of protest. When none came she hurriedly restored the ball to its bag and the backpack, and presently her heart and thoughts slowed and she decided that the experience with the ball hadn't happened.

There was silence in the grove, and Hazel stood to regard the tree nearest her. With doctoring could it really be made healthy again? Grow oranges? If that was possible, then she could, sure enough, become rich. With the money she'd get for the grove she would be able to buy not just plain gold earrings, but a pair that dangled with pounds of diamonds. And the purple, rocket-shaped car wouldn't be the only one she would own. She would buy two, but the second one would be silver and not shaped like a car. It would only be half car. The half that wasn't car would be a machine that would pull in its wheels when a button was pushed and gallop down the road on legs. She would hire somebody to invent it. The purple car would be the one for her private use, and the one with the legs would be the one she would use in a taxi business. Everybody would want to ride in it and they wouldn't care how much she charged.

Hazel smiled her red-and-white smile and watched Felder coming back through the grove carrying the shovel. Having made a big decision, she was at her most gracious and humble while selecting a burial site for the box of garbage. Unaccustomed to the ways of courting a friendship, she complimented Felder on his abilities as a hole digger and garbage dumper. "Did you like my house?" she asked.

"Sure I did," answered Felder. "It's got almost everything anybody would want. I only saw one fault with it."

"A fault? What fault?"

"It hasn't got a swimming pool."

"A swimming pool," croaked Hazel. "You thought you'd see a swimming pool? To go with that tacky house? Listen here, where do you think you are?"

"I know where I am," said Felder, "but I don't know if you do. What shall I do with this leftover dirt?"

"Spread it around," said Hazel. "Look here, Felder, my brother's got a swimming pool at his house and do you know how much it cost him? Thousands. And it takes thousands of gallons of water to fill it up. He had to sink a well."

"You've got a well," reported Felder. "And if I had to guess if it's shallow or deep, I'd say deep. There's a pump to go with it. I looked."

"About that swimming pool," blathered Hazel. "If you lived in that house would you really have to have it? Couldn't you put two washerwoman tubs together and swim in those? There are a couple of real nice ones somebody left in my house. The washerwoman kind. If you painted their insides blue and pushed dirt up around them, they'd look like a swimming pool, wouldn't they?"

"Oh, sure they would," responded Felder. "Your brother should have thought of that. It would have saved him all those thousands he spent on his pool."

"Two of those round tubs like poor people use when they do their wash would be big enough for you to flop around in whenever you felt like a swim," reasoned Hazel. "If you lived in my house and just had to have a swimming pool, that's what you could do. Personally I don't care for swimming pools. They stink like cleaning stuff. When I want a swim I go to our creek. It's so dry now the fish are coughing up sand, but pretty soon it'll rain and then it will fill up again."

"I don't live in your house," said Felder with an eye to what lay beyond the grove and the grove house. In the distant forest, the climax forest where the land on which it stood offered hospitality only to seed of its own tree kind, the sun glowed. Between the oaks there were aisles of shade, and east and west of the trees there were little areas of sand soaks, pools of coarse white sand useless to citrus cultivation.

"I say I don't live in your house," repeated Felder. He stood the shovel in the ground and went to his backpack to kneel, to open the pack. His hand went to the bag containing the ball. He held it up, discovered its wound, and instantly his anger flamed. "My puffball. Left over from last year. You shouldn't have cut it. Why did you?"

At a loss to explain her sinful act, Hazel looked at Felder as she looked at her father when trusting him to solve for her a troublesome problem or a mystery. She could not put into words the attraction she had felt for the ball, nor the strange excitement and disturbance she had felt when it had sighed and opened and spewed its queer, smokelike cloud. "I don't know why I did it," she confessed, hiding her feelings. "It made me feel funny and I wanted to see what it would do if I cut it, that's all. Should I pay you for it? I'll pay you for it."

Said Felder in a curt tone, "I don't collect things like puffballs to sell."

"What do you collect them for?"

"Aw," said Felder, "why do you want to know?"

"I just do," replied Hazel. "I never saw a puffball before."

Felder's ire melted. "I collect things like puffballs for me. To study. As soon as we find a place to live, I'm going to look for some kind of a job I can do this summer, and with the money I make, I'm going to buy a microscope."

"Why?"

"So I can see what I collect better. That's what a microscope is for. Haven't you ever looked at anything through one?"

"I might have," evaded Hazel, concealing her ignorance of microscopes. "All those seeds and other stuff in those jars and bags are just for you to look at? What about those sticks, and what's that stuff they're in?"

"Those aren't just plain sticks. They're bud sticks, and the stuff around them is sphagnum moss. Yesterday we were up the Ridge a way helping a man with his grove work, and when he paid us, he gave me this bundle. They're to put in tree sprouts, to make them grow fruit again."

Hazel glanced at her feet. In their black school shoes they were firm on the ground, yet she felt as though they had become unhinged from her legs and were carrying her forward on tiptoe to a shore of some kind. The odor of the puffball's vapor was still in her nose, still clung to her fingers, and this boy Felder with his tastes in the different might be one of those who would plod away at something until either he dropped or was told to quit, but he was also the kind that could head things up, take charge. Like the teacher at school, the one who sat scrawling her dreams out the window, but who could turn and in just a second make everybody jump up and scream out answers to questions she hadn't even asked.

Hazel moved to stand beside Felder, to watch his hands busy with the backpack, rearranging and securing his precious treasures. He looked up at her and said, "What? What now?"

"The grove," huffed Hazel. "You said you could make it grow again. If you could, and if you would, I'd let you and your mama and sisters live in my house free."

Felder's impassive face remained so. "For how long?"

"For as long as it would take to make it look like a grove again. So when somebody with some money comes along, they'll be crazy about it and won't be able to haul their money out fast enough."

"It would take a while and some cash," said Felder after a moment.

Hard eyed, Hazel said, "How long is a while?"

"Months."

"And how much money? What would you need money for?"

"Fertilizer. These trees should be fertilized now, and when I cut back all the dead branches and twigs, I should spray for insects. Did you say you had some money?"

Hazel ate pride. "No, I didn't say I had some money, but I'll get some from somewhere. My dad might lend me some. Or my brother. My brother has gobs of money and I think he'd help me. What else?"

"My mother," said Felder. "I'll have to ask my mother about this. I'm man of our family now, but she's still the boss."

"Do you think she'll say yes?"

"Maybe. She likes us to live in the country, and this is country."

"Listen," said Hazel. "How can you be so calm? I'm handing you a present. Your mother said the reason you all stopped here was because you wanted to rent the grove house, and I'm offering it to you now free just for fixing up my grove. And now you say maybe. Maybe why?"

"Maybe," said Felder, "I'd want some of what you get out of the grove when you sell it."

"Yes, yes, of course you would. I meant to say that."

"Ten percent," insisted Felder.

"Yes, yes, ten percent," agreed Hazel, though she had only a faint notion of what this part of the bargain meant. To her, percentages of anything were as alien as the location of Norway or the Amazon jungles.

Felder offered a sly challenge. "I don't believe you can do it. Kids no older than we are can't own big things like groves and houses."

"Why can't we?"

"Because it's not legal."

"What's legal?"

"Legal is law."

"My dad is my law," stated Hazel. "He gave me this grove and that house, and said I could do anything I wanted to with it."

"Your dad," countered Felder, "said he didn't want us here. He said he wouldn't rent us the house. What's he going to say when you tell him you've rented it to us?"

"Oh, a lot," answered Hazel, uttering what she knew to be a simple, solid, and interesting prospect. Interesting because the word fights between her and her father were seldom on a simple scale. Usually they were so grand that her mother would toss a nightgown and a toothbrush and some other personal things in a bag and tear off down the road to throw herself on the mercies of Donnie and Vannie Lee.

"He'll squawk," said Hazel, "and maybe he'll break some dishes or go out and beat on the fence, but that won't last long and he won't be mad at you. It'll all be at me, and that won't last long either. As soon as he remembers what he said when he gave me the grove and the house, he'll get over being mad. He's a sweet man and he's always fair." Sure of herself, and with fresh vision, she turned and observed the tree nearest her. In her mind its dead branches fell away and new ones shot out from its trunk, green of leaf and heavy with fruit. She saw the whole grove that way, three acres of growing gold.

2

So now for Hazel this time and its matters were met, and in their clamor she ran in yellow sunlight, leaving the grove behind, leaving Felder to dawdle, to investigate, so curious about all. So hopeful yet still unconvinced that this broken-down domain was to be his for a while to live in, to restore.

In the Ryes' kitchen Hazel's mother sat at the cleared table, drinking coffee and playing with a slice of toast. The room had received and was still receiving a powerful surprise. The stove's top and front were white again, as were the cabinet doors. In their rack the bathed dishes stood air drying, and on their hands and knees Jo Poole and her girls were working on the floor as though it might be a live enemy and they intended either to suffocate it or drown it. Scrubbing and wiping they dipped their brushes and rags into buckets of soapy water and Jo said, "Soon as we get all this soap worked in good, we'll bring the hose in from the outside and rinse it all out. I don't know about laying down a coat of wax though. We won't have time for that. It will take this floor at least an hour to dry."

Hazel offered her surprise. "You'll have time. I've decided to rent you my grove house if you still want it. I'm going out and tell my dad in a minute."

A little moan escaped Ona Rye's mouth. "Oh," she said. "Oh."

"She's not feeling well," said Jo, addressing Hazel. "Watch where you walk, honey. This is dangerous territory right now. Go sit by your mama why don't you? No, not on the table, dear. Jewel just cleaned it. Take a chair."

"If you still want to rent my house, it won't cost you anything," said Hazel. "Felder's going to be my business partner and fix up my grove so I can get more money for it when I sell it. What he does for me will be my rent money."

"I don't know what's wrong with me," said Ona Rye. "Neither does my doctor." Her nose was too prominent for the rest of her face and her words came from her as though being pulled.

"Maybe you don't eat enough," sympathized Jo. "You look like you ought to be carrying an anchor around with you to keep you from blowing away."

"Last Tuesday when I was to see my doctor, he said I should get away from here for a while, and I've been thinking about that," said Hazel's mother. "My folks live in Tennessee and I think it would do me good to see them again."

"I've never been to see Tennessee," remarked Jo Poole. "But I've read about it."

"I don't like to read," said Ona. "It gives me the headache." With an expression of apprehension, she slid her glance toward Hazel. "I have a headache now."

Hazel leaned to pat her mother's hand. She spoke to Jo Poole's back. "I guess you didn't hear me when I said you could rent my house. You still want it, don't you?"

Rising from her floor task, Jo came to the table.

"Yes, we do, but I don't know about this arrangement between you and Felder. How do you think your father is going to take this? He said he didn't want us here."

"That was before Felder and I went and looked at my grove," reasoned Hazel. "Now it's different. As soon as I go out and talk to him, he'll want you here. I want you here. So will my dad as soon as I tell him what all Felder is going to do for me."

"That Felder," said Jo. "That Felder." And from some brambled corner in the yard, a wild, winged thing whistled a note of triumph.

In his chair on the porch, Millard Rye took the news concerning Hazel's new tenants as if he might be listening to some idea uttered by a lunatic. First came his silent show of disbelief, then a pitying smile, then a fatherly hug for one whose ignorance was to be forgiven. And at last a silent war with patience and then a rush of patience gone athwart.

As scenes of this nature always did, this one began with an exhibition of something-in-the-wind innocence.

Said Hazel, "Mama might go to Tennessee and stay with Grandpa and Grandma for a while."

"She told me," said Millard. "Are them people back there in the kitchen about through?"

"No."

"What're they doing?"

"Washing everything."

"I knew the minute I laid my eyes on that woman she had a cleaning disease," commented Millard. "Is that boy of hers helping?"

"No."

"I thought he'd be the kind that would."

"He's out in the grove now. Looking things over. He collects things. Have you ever cut a puffball open and smelled what's inside it?"

"Not me."

"It makes you think of things far away. I wonder what makes a puffball. I forgot to ask Felder. You don't happen to know, do you?"

"I'm afraid not. I got more important things to do with my time than run around sniffing puffballs. Is that kid's name really Felder? I wasn't listening too hard when he was introduced."

"Yah," said Hazel. "That's his name. Felder. And he's smart."

"Felder," said Millard. "Well, I guess one more problem like his name won't hurt him."

Hazel skipped to the far end of the porch and wrapped her arms around one of its poles. "I went with him out to my grove to bury some garbage.

He says he can make my trees grow again, so when I sell my grove I can get more money for it. He's going to live in my house while he's doing it, him and his mama and sisters. I rented it to them. I told them they wouldn't have to pay me anything. Getting the grove fixed up like new again will be my pay."

Millard Rye stood and sat again. He faced her, and the workings of his mind peeped at her. "You did that without so much as a by-your-leave from me? After we both told them we didn't want them here? Why'd you do that?"

Gently reproving, Hazel said, "It was the grove. I want it to grow oranges again. I don't see why you're mad."

With a fixed, glassy focus Millard said, "I'm mad at you for going behind my back. You've never done that before. Did you tell your mama?"

"She knows about it."

"What'd she say?"

"She said she had a headache. What do you mean, I went behind your back?"

"You sneaked around in back of me and cooked all of this up without telling me first," said Millard, gearing up for a fight. "That's what I'm mad about.

I'm surprised. It hurts me. You in love with that pole?"

Hazel backed away from the pole and, dangerously experimenting, dipped into her own pot of fight. "I have never sneaked around in back of you to do anything. Never. I don't sneak around, and you ought to be ashamed of yourself for saying I did."

Her father's retort was cold. "I'll say anything I want to say. I'm your dad. The trouble with you is, I let you forget that too often."

"The grove," said Hazel, nimbly dipping deeper, "is mine, and so is the house in it. You gave it to me and said I could do anything I wanted to with it. Don't you remember?"

"I remember."

"Well, then."

"The trouble with you," dodged Millard Rye, "is I've always been too good to you. Some fathers tie their little bad children up in the yard like dogs and leave them there all day to learn them how to behave and have respect for their daddies. Did you know that?"

"If you ever tied me up like a dog and left me in the yard all day, I'd get loose and run so far away you'd never see me again," threatened Hazel.

"It's all my fault," ranted her father. "I'm to blame. Not any of the way you are is your fault. It's all mine. I've always given you everything and never asked you to give me anything back except be my friend."

"I'm your friend."

"Some friend. You don't even know when my birthday is. The last time it came around I had to tell you, and you didn't even wish me a happy one. That takes gall. Wouldn't you say that takes gall?"

"Yes, Millard," said Hazel. "I'd say it does."

"But you got lots of that, haven't you?"

"I guess I've got enough."

"I guess you have too. I'll tell you what I've got. I've got a couple of orders for you."

"All right, Millard."

"From now on, you don't call me by my first name. I'm your dad and that's what you can call me. You got that?"

"Yes, Dad."

"Or you can call me sir."

"All right, sir."

"It's going to take a little money for you and your hired hand to fix up your grove. Have you thought about that?"

"Yes, sir. I have. A little."

"That's going to be your worry. Don't you come whining to me about it. And don't you go to my pants' pockets and help yourself to what's in them either like I've always let you do before. Or go bellyaching to your mama or Donnie for a loan. School's out now so I won't be giving you your lunch money. I'll only be giving you your regular allowance, but from now on if you run out ahead of time, don't you count on me for any more. You can get out and earn what you need. Or go rob a bank. That's what I'd have to do if I was in your place."

"You want me to rob a bank?" asked Hazel, incredulous. "Sir, I can't do that. I don't know how."

"Oh, good grief a-mercy," exclaimed Millard Rye. "Naturally I don't want you to rob a bank. Robbing banks is what puts people in prisons and cemeteries. I don't want you to rob a bank. I just said that. What I want you to do is forget this whole deal. It's not a good one. That kid Felder don't know no more about raising oranges than I do, and what I know about it, you could put in a flea's eye. So don't you think you ought to forget it?"

"No, sir," said Hazel. "Unless when you told

me the house and the grove were mine to do what I wanted to with them was a lie."

Hazel's father hesitated not more than two seconds. He came up out of his chair, lifted it, and hurled it into the yard. Upright, it landed in a clump of thick, prickly bushes; and Millard Rye left the porch in a leap, ran to the chair, hauled it from the bushes, raised it by one of its arms, and slammed it against the brick walk.

Hazel's mother had come to the door to stand in its case, and although she was pale, there was fire in her eyes.

Said Hazel, "Don't shake, Mama. That's what he wants you to do, so he can say I caused it. He's just having one of his spasms. He'll be over it in a minute. It wasn't my fault this time. You want me to help you to your room?"

"No, I don't want you to help me to my room," answered Ona Rye. "Take your dirty little hands off me and go phone Donnie and tell him to come get me. If he's not home, tell Vannie Lee to come, and right away. I want either her or Donnie to take me to the airport. I'm going to Tennessee. Now. Today. On the next plane."

"Dad," screamed Hazel. "Mama's going to Tennessee. Today. On the next plane. You'd better come and tell her good-bye. You've done enough to that chair now. Come on, sir. Be nice. Mama's going, and if you don't come and tell her good-bye before she leaves, you'll be sorry."

Through with the injured chair, which lay on its side, Millard gave it a final kick, went striding to his truck which was parked just outside the front gate, jumped in it, and drove off.

"What a terrible temper," murmured Hazel. "He'd better be careful. You remember Mr. Jenkins, Mama?"

"Oh," said her mother, "don't tell me about Mr. Jenkins again. It wasn't his temper that caused him to have his stroke. It was his arteries."

In her bedroom while Hazel watched, she filled two suitcases and a tote bag, and when Vannie Lee came for her, she was ready to go. To Vannie Lee she said, "If one of them kills the other while I'm gone, just you and Donnie bury the dead one and don't call to tell me which one it is. I don't care anymore."

"Nobody's going to kill anybody while you're gone," soothed Vannie Lee, stowing the suitcases and the tote bag in the trunk of her car. She was dressed for the trip to the nearest airport in a tight orange suit and wanted to know what all the commotion in the kitchen was about.

"Ask Hazel," said Ona Rye. "But not now. Let's go." At the last minute she accepted Hazel's kiss and a farewell present, a potholder hand stitched and restitched at great pain under the pitying eye of Vannie Lee. The holder was lumpy, not the product of anyone talented in the ways of needle and thread.

Standing alone on the porch watching her mother being whisked away, Hazel suffered a short and frightening breakdown, one that surpassed all others she had experienced. Her faults gathered in her mind and hung themselves up in an honest line, and for their ugliness, she wept behind locked hands. To her tears she added private apologies, offering them to the empty road, to the lonely sky, to the assaulted chair.

The chair was light, and she dragged it up the walk and the steps and set it in its usual place. Examining its damage, she spoke to it out of a full and guilty heart. "Since Donnie got married, I'm all they've got left and I've got to stop being so mean and hateful to them. So selfish. They give me everything, and all I give them back is trouble."

She sat in the chair with a hand on its broken arm and listened to the voices and the sounds of cleaning coming through the house from the kitchen. She couldn't make out what it was the Pooles talked about with such energy. There was laughter, and presently she went inside to her room. When she returned to the porch, she was freshly dressed. From the porch railing she watched the road for her father, and when she saw his square, closed truck appear on the curve in the road, she moved to the steps and sat down on the top one.

Her father only glanced at the Pooles' car and trailer. He had brought Hazel a box of peanut brittle and a comic book, and as if nothing was amiss between them said, "I waited for Vannie Lee at Sperry's Corner so I could tell your mama good-bye. One of these days I'm going to have to get up enough nerve to speak to Vannie Lee about the way she gets herself up. That suit she's got on today fits her like a drink of water."

"Vannie Lee is good," declared Hazel, rushing toward a royal goal. "When her mother and father come to visit her and Donnie, she always treats them like they aren't even kin to her. She's never ugly to them the way I'm ugly to you and Mama sometimes. While you were gone I decided I'd try to be like her. Do you know every time she tells her mother and father good-bye, she kisses them and tells them she loves them? I think that's sweet, don't you?"

"I don't know if I do or if I don't," said Millard Rye. "I never have wanted my kids to slobber over me."

"I wouldn't ever slobber over you. I'd just let you know I loved you."

"I know you love me."

"Thank you for the comic book and candy."

"You're welcome."

"I won't forget your birthday again. Next time it comes, I'm going to find out about it ahead of time and do something special for you like Vannie Lee does for her dad on his birthday. She's nice."

"Yes, she's nice," agreed Millard.

Hazel proclaimed that life had surely changed. "I've decided I won't rent my house to the Pooles. It wouldn't be legal."

Her declaration, so well intentioned, missed its target. Instantly Millard Rye said, "Wouldn't be legal? Who says so?"

"Felder."

"Felder. Is Felder a lawyer?"

"No, but I think he knows about a lot of stuff.

He studies things. And as soon as he gets some money, he's going to buy a microscope so he can study them better. I think he must be very smart."

"Smart or not smart," said Millard, "he's still not a lawyer. I gave you the grove and the grove house and told you you could do with it what you wanted and that's all the legal you need."

Fuddled, Hazel took what she thought might be the right road to peace. "But I want to mind you, sir. Obey you, that's what I meant to say. I want to obey you. I'm not going to be bad anymore. I'm going to be good. When you tell me to do something, I'm going to do it. Right then. Yes, I'll do it. After this, I'll do everything you say."

Into her father's face there came at once an untidy look. It revealed his weakest spot. "I don't want you to always do everything I say. If you did, pretty soon I'd start to thinking you had lost some of your biscuits. You got to be yourself, lady. I know that. Now, about them people back there in the kitchen. If you've already struck up a bargain with them, you shouldn't go back on your word."

"You are right, sir," said Hazel. "You are right."

"I see you got on your regular buddy clothes, so why don't we take us a ride somewhere? I tell you what. As soon as the Pooles finish up with whatever they're doing, they can go on to the grove house and let's you and me go to town and each of us get us a big, sloppy sandwich and some popcorn and we'll go to a picture show. For our supper we'll eat us a steak at Bernie's. Your mama won't be there to watch, so we can have Bernie fix them like we want them. Rare."

"The grove," said Hazel.

"It's not going anyplace," said Millard. "It'll be here when you get back."

"Yes, but it'll be dark," protested Hazel. "While we're gone, Felder might want to do some work in it, and I want to stay here and watch. He's got some bud sticks. They're not just plain sticks. They're what you put in tree sprouts to make them grow fruit again."

Not by look or word did Millard Rye oppose this piece of information. The Pooles had all come to the door and were standing crowded within its embrasure, waiting to be recognized. Hazel's father turned his head to silently observe them. When his gaze rested on Felder, he produced a smile which advanced a slow strain. It was the guarded and jealous smile of the rivaled.

3

To the startled house in the grove went the rambunctious and delighted Pooles, and out of their hauling trailer came the tools and properties of homekeeping. As though working from a blueprint, they went about conquering smut and grime and tangle. Jo produced a loaf of bread, and on the run, Hazel's tenants ate this and the donated Rye ham, chasing the salty, sawed-off chunks with many glasses of water.

Jo said she was relieved to see that there was working electricity in the house. Wanda said about all she could say for the water was that it was wet. And Felder went outside to the well's holding tank, opened its valves, and allowed the stored water to spill out onto the ground until it ran clear and free of sediment. If there were qualms concerning the kitchen appliances and the scarred furniture, the Pooles kept these to themselves.

To Hazel, spectator to all of the carrying in and carrying out, the whole scurrying pursuit was an annoyance that she tried disguising. In a fervor to get to the more important work, the grove work, she trailed around with first one Poole and then another, heartily agreeing with every notion and arrangement. Or disagreeing, if disagreement meant progress. In one of the two bedrooms she watched Wanda hang a small mirror. "All of you know how to do everything and you do it so quick," she cheered.

"We're a nation," declared Wanda.

"You aren't Americans? I thought you were Americans."

"We are, but we're still a nation."

"What kind?"

"Oh," said Wanda, "if I told you, you wouldn't

know any more than if I hadn't, so let's not talk about that now. If we stay here long enough, you'll find out what kind. Does this mirror look like it's hung right to you?"

"Yes, yes, it's just right. Don't change it. Why can't you go clean the bathroom now so Felder won't have to do it? That's not a boy job."

To better survey her handiwork Wanda stood back from the mirror. "The bathroom is Felder's job if Mama said it was and she did."

Hazel lodged a protest. "These things all of you are doing now weren't in my bargain. My bargain was for Felder to get out there and get my trees to growing again."

"Oh, don't be so petty," said Wanda. "Relax. That's such a nice little television set out in the front room. Why don't you go and watch a program?"

"I don't want to watch a program," said Hazel. "I get enough of those at home."

"Then read a book while you're waiting," suggested Wanda. "Look. There are stacks of them here."

"I don't care much for books," said Hazel, eyeing both Wanda and her books with disdain.

"I'm so sorry," said Wanda. "That's sad."

"I think books are dumber than tacks and people who sit around reading them all the time are sapwits."

"Well," said Wanda, "at least the way you word your opinions shows originality. I am impressed."

"I know what originality is because I'm original," said Hazel. Wanda's plain face and sandpiper legs made her think of her teacher, and her heart skipped a couple of hostile beats. "My dad doesn't read books, and neither does my brother, but they both make plenty of money."

"Money, money," said Wanda with lifted eyes. "It's glorious. I wish I had some. I wonder if I'm wasting my life."

"I don't know," said Hazel, "but you'd better think about it before you get old. I know an old man in Echo Spring and he's got a whole room full of books, but it looks to me like they haven't done him much good. He makes quilts to rest his mind and lives all by himself and bellers a lot."

"He does what, Hazel?"

"Bellers. At kids when they write bad words on his fence. *Baaaaw!* Like that. But he never does that to me. I don't write bad words on his fence. He likes to talk to me and show me things. He's got the biggest house and the biggest yard in Echo

Spring and weeds that eat flies. His name is Mr. Bartlett, and he likes my brain. One time he told me he'd give ten thousand dollars to have a brain like mine."

Asked Wanda, "What does this Mr. Bartlett do besides read and make quilts and feed flies to weeds?"

"Plants things. Watches for me so when I go past his house he can come out and talk to me. He said he'd give ten thousand dollars to have a brain like mine, but he'd only pay a hundred dollars to have one like Jimmy Kitchen's. Ha! I guess I showed up old Jimmy that time. He laughed so hard he fell down on the sidewalk, but he didn't think it was funny. He was just putting on. His silly brain is only worth a hundred dollars and mine is worth ten thousand. What do you think about that?"

With a catch in her voice Wanda answered, "I'm not sure. I'd like to know the difference between your brain and Jimmy's. There must be a big one."

Endlessly fond of the memory, Hazel reflected. "Mr. Bartlett said Jimmy's brain had been used too much but mine is like new. I told my dad about it."

"And what did he say?"

"He laughed," answered Hazel. She was gratified to see Wanda's eyes widen, but it was not for Wanda's admiration that she thirsted. It was for action.

Her thirst was not to be satisfied with the hoped-for speed. First came Felder's cool preparations: the selection of tools taken from the grove house and now resting on the Pooles' back porch, a studious review of pages in the citrus books, the emptying of Felder's backpack down to the knife, the swatch of budding tapes, and the bundled bud sticks still safely moist in their nest of moss inside the plastic bag.

Of the bud sticks Felder said, "We'll need more of these, but we won't worry about that today."

Felder moved with method. In the grove, in the warmth of the four-o'clock stillness, he loped from tree to tree, diagnosing and talking to himself. He was untouched by Hazel's shrill urgings.

A wind ran through the waiting trees and some of them rattled their skeleton arms.

"Terrible," mourned Hazel. "Just terrible."

Felder turned a clear look on her. "Good creeps almighty, you don't know what terrible is. Here. Grab hold of this hoe and start loosening the dirt up around these first two trees here. Don't dig.

Go at it easy. Think you can do that?"

Astonished, Hazel jumped to the job of setting her employee straight. "Did you say you wanted me to dig up the dirt around these trees? Me? While you do what? Listen here, Felder, I'm the boss so I'm the one supposed to give the orders. Not you."

Felder was not amused nor was he insulted. Promptly he became the corrected employee who knew that he had got off on the wrong foot with management. Agreeably, hoe in hand, he went to the first of the trees and began a careful tillage, working around the crown of the root system, loosening the earth and opening it, moving around and around until a spread of about three feet out from the tree's trunk had been cultivated. There was nothing in the sight of this to stir the heart.

Finished with the first of the trees, Felder moved to the next one and lingered over three green shoots grown out from its trunk. Two were spindly. The third appeared vigorous. Above these there were gray, dead branches, and Felder, steering a bland and respectful course, asked, "What you want me to do about this tree?"

Hazel issued a hard order. "Make it grow. That's what you're here for."

"It's growing now."

"Just the bottom. The top looks awful. Awful. Fix it."

"How?"

"Felder, I don't know how. You said you did."

"There's something wrong with my memory. I noticed that just a couple of minutes ago. It's not working. Should I prune off all these dead branches?"

"Sure."

"And then some new ones will grow out of the trunk, won't they?"

"Sure."

"Won't that be a miracle."

"New branches won't come?"

"Not above the freeze line they won't."

"Not ever?"

"I didn't say that."

"What did you say?"

Felder's quick glance reduced her to a child's nuisance size. "Boss, I think I have made a mistake and what I'd better do about it is get on back and tell my mother and sisters about it before I get in any deeper. Would you mind carrying the hoe? It's not very heavy. And would you mind if I helped myself to this little weed here? I'm mad for weeds.

Do you know that the seed that made this one might have come thousands of miles before it landed here?"

"You're quitting me?" shrieked Hazel. "But you haven't hardly got started yet."

"I got started," said Felder, pushing his hands into the soil to loosen and lift his weed.

The westering sun had begun to take on its late-afternoon color, and out over the climax forest some big birds passed and repassed. The grove sighed, and there was a moment of tension between its two human occupants before Hazel gave into it. "Well, thunder," she said, "if you wanted to be the boss why didn't you say so? I don't care. You can be the boss and I'll be your helper. What you want me to do first?"

Felder considered, and after another moment and then another had gone he said, "Stand there. Stand there or sit there and be quiet. Can you do that?"

"Yes," said Hazel and sat on the ground watching, watching.

In Felder's hands the saw and the hand clippers did their work, and presently the first of the trees to undergo surgery stood properly shorn, the area to be budded cleaned of thorns and twigs. Two of the tree's spindly shoots, those grown out from its ground crown, had not been spared. The most vigorous one waited to receive new life, the insertion of a single bud now attached to a piece of bark, well developed but still dormant.

The cut on the shoot was made, the bud was placed in the incision, the wrapping, securing bud to shoot, was done. Soon, with luck, under the strip of the budding tape, under one of the polyethylene strips, there would take place a union between the bud and the parent stock.

Hazel viewed all of this with the eyes of the amateur discovering that she no longer wishes to be one. Within her a clean and eerie passion had begun to punch and thump. Young and ignorant and far afield, it did not speak its meaning. The feeling that she was being turned, that she was under some kind of attack, rolled through her, and now there was no thought of what the trees might do for her. There was only the feeling of being related to earthy things and of being pushed into a new and marvelously mystifying place.

There was dust in her mouth and she swallowed it, and as if she would take some of its magical growing power to herself, she moved closer to the sealed bud in the shoot. "Oh, I like it," she said. "Isn't it sweet? Just like a little baby."

Preparing to go on to the next tree, Felder gathered up his tools. "Yup, it's got a new mama now, and they're going to like each other. In about two or three weeks I'll take the wrapping off and then you'll see. Bring the bud sticks, but be careful how you handle them because we haven't got any to waste. You don't happen to know somebody who would give us some more, do you?"

Thankful to be relieved of her employer role, Hazel lifted the bud sticks. "I know Mr. Bartlett in Echo Spring. He's got a grove out in back of his house. He likes me, so tomorrow I'll ask my brother's wife to take me to his house and I'll see if he's got any extra. You can go with me if you want to. Give me the hoe and I'll go on ahead and dig around the rest of the trees in this row while you stay here and do what you have to do."

Now there was agreement between the leader and the led, the two in the grove working steadily until the last tree in the first row had been barbered and the last of the buds lay firm in its new womb.

The afternoon was drawing toward its close. In the coming dusk Hazel followed Felder from the grove, intending only to stop long enough at the Poole's place for a little rest and a glass of water. She was dirtied and tired as she had never been, and she sat in the Pooles' kitchen, hugging her satisfaction and her inner altered being. She watched Jo Poole create a large, canned-meat pie with materials taken from the Pooles' meager store of dried and canned foodstuffs. She said, "We never have that at home. My mother is a terrible cook, especially on Sundays. That's when she has her worst headaches, so my dad and I usually go to Echo Spring and get us a little old sloppy something to eat and take it to the picture show with us. After that we go to Bernie's and eat us a steak. I'm my dad's best buddy."

Jo spread a sheet of dough over the pan of meat pie, and with a knife slashed some vent holes in it. "Do you think your dad would like to come and take supper with us?"

"He might, but he's gone to Echo Spring."

"Then will you stay and eat with us?"

"Will there be enough to go around?"

"Oh, yes, and then some. For our dessert we'll have some raisins. Would you like to get rid of some of that dirt on your face and hands before we eat?"

"No, I'm fine like I am," answered Hazel, in love with her dirt, in love with the old raftered kitchen, in love with the hour.

When the pie came from the oven and supper was called, she observed how Felder and his sisters respectfully stood behind their chairs until their mother was seated. She watched as the Pooles bowed their heads and listened as Jo Poole asked God to bless the food they were about to receive and to thank Him for it and all their blessings.

There was table talk, and during lags in it Hazel took potshots at joining it with some observations of her own, but the Pooles were too much ahead of her. They knew about the world, its seas and mountains and mesas, its sciences. Their conversations took them out of themselves and away from the grove house. They spoke of the why and how of things and jabbered of the places and styles they had actually seen and of those known only to them by way of what they had read about in their books. There were disputes settled by racing trips to a big dictionary and other volumes of reference. Led by Jo Poole, the discussions were spirited and loud and there was high-faring in them, and family bond.

Hazel watched their antics and listened to their noises. She ate her portion of the raisins and went home and sat with her father on the Ryes' front porch.

Millard Rye looked at her dirt and fatigue and

passed a comment. "Lady, you look like you had a day of it, sure enough."

"Yes, sir," said Hazel. "I had a day of it, sure enough."

"You got blisters?"

"A couple."

"They hurt?"

"No, sir."

"Mine always hurt."

"Mine don't."

"You learn all about grove caring today?"

"No, not all of it. A lot though."

"Hard work, isn't it?"

"Yes, sir."

"You ready to give it up?"

"No, sir."

Millard Rye lifted a foot and removed one shoe and one sock. "You had your supper?"

"I ate with the Pooles. We had meat pie and raisins. Good."

"After my movie I had me a good thick steak at Bernie's," said Hazel's father. "He wanted to know where you was, and I told him you had quit me and taken up with the Pooles."

"I haven't quit you," said Hazel.

"Haven't you? Well, maybe I just dreamed I had to go to the picture show and eat my supper by myself. Let me tell you something I hadn't ever told you before. I quit my daddy when I was nine year old. It wasn't a case of have to. He owned a grocery store, so we always had us plenty to eat, but one day we had a argument over some little old something I wanted to do and he didn't want me to do, and I got it into my head I was smarter than him, so I quit him."

"Where did you go?"

"I didn't go nowheres. I kept on living with him till the law said I was old enough to leave school and go to work, but after our argument that day, he went his way and I went mine. Whenever I think of the way we used to pass days without saying a word to each other, I'm a little bit sorry. It's natural and a good thing for a young one to want to get out and earn his own money and be his own boss, but he shouldn't ever haul off and quit his daddy or say he's smarter."

"I haven't quit you, and I don't think I'm smarter than you," said Hazel. "But I can't be two places at the same time, and today I wanted to work with Felder in my grove."

"Did you say you learned all about it?"

"No, sir, I didn't say that. I said I learned a lot, not all."

"I'll lay you five-to-one-on odds you didn't learn berries from Felder today about how to treat a froze grove," said Millard Rye. "Be honest now."

"Felder didn't talk to me about berries," said Hazel. "He talked about how to bud trees, except when we were having our supper. Then he talked about everything, and so did everybody else. The Pooles have got about a ton of books, and when they don't know something, they run to their books and look it up. They've got a big dictionary."

Hazel's father bent to remove his other shoe and sock. "About the Pooles."

"Yes, sir?"

"I wouldn't like it if you got too thick with them. They are not our kind."

"I know that already," said Hazel.

Night had come, and through the trees in the grove she could see a prick of light dimly shining from one of the Pooles' windows. There were patches of light too above the grove, patches of stars serenely glittering. How old were they and how far away? And how was it she had never wondered about them before?

"When I come in from work tomorrow evening, remind me to fix this chair," said Millard Rye.

"I'll remind you," said Hazel.

In the darkness of the porch she sat looking at the stars and tried not to hear her father, now in a lighter mood, describe the movie he had seen that afternoon. All about how the bad guy almost got away and how the good guy won.

4

Millard Rye was not a noticer of either big or little miracles, and so to him, the coming of a new day was but a plain and reliable fact. On this Monday morning in his plain and reliable kitchen, he fried bacon and carefully heartened the heat under the omelet.

At the table, waiting to be served, Hazel said, "I dreamed last night I was somebody else. Did you ever do that?"

"No," answered her father. "I never wanted to be nobody else so I never thought about it so I never dreamed it." He brought the omelet and a pan of bakery doughnuts to the table, filled Hazel's plate and his own, sat down, and said, "Eat."

"You too," said Hazel.

"What you got mapped out for yourself today?"

"I'm going to town with Vannie Lee if she goes."

"You want to ride down as far as her house with me?"

"No. She'll come after me if I phone her and ask her, but I can't do that now because she never gets up this early, and besides I have to go and see Felder about some things."

"The Pooles breezed out of here about an hour ago," said Millard Rye.

"They left?" said Hazel. "All of them?"

"I didn't count heads," answered her father. He ate quickly, and when his plate was clean said, "Come give your old dad a smoochie. I've got to get going myself."

The day was young, and standing on the porch, watching her father drive away, Hazel felt its coming warmth. In the grove the night mists were blowing out, and beyond them the white moon was quitting the horizon.

From out of the mists came Felder, cleanly clothed, head up, stepping briskly. His backpack was slung from one shoulder, and in a fury of relief Hazel ran to meet him. "My dad said he saw all of you breeze out of here about an hour ago and I was worried. You're not supposed to worry me. You're not supposed to forget me and your job. Did you just happen to remember us and come back?"

"Woman," said Felder. "Oh, woman."

"Well," screeched Hazel, "some people forget what they say they'll do. I used to. One time when I was in second grade I was supposed to be a sunbonnet babe in one of their ninny plays, but I forgot to tell my mother, so she didn't get me a watering can or anybody to make my costume, so instead I had to be a fence post. They put a big brown paper bag over me, and I had to stand on the stage and not move, and I got so hot under that bag I like to have died. See what I mean?"

Felder was looking at her as if she might be a symptom of something in need of attention. "Mama and Wanda went to Echo Spring to look for jobs and they took Jewel with them. I was taking a bath when they left. What about your brother's wife?

Is she coming after us to take us where we're going?''

"No," replied Hazel. "What we're going to do is hot-track it down to her house and wait for her to get out of bed and get herself all prissied up to go to town so she can take her dancing lesson and her ceramic lesson. That'll be quicker than waiting for her here."

Out on the road she was required to run and skip and run again in order to keep up with Felder's quick gait. He talked of the lack of rain and a trouble new to her, leaf wilting in some of her trees, those that the original owner had wisely planted on the rise of land between the grove house and the protecting highland forest. Thick-barked old warriors these, they had come through the past winter's freeze with less injury than had their more youthful kin. Felder said that if it did not rain soon, the time would come when the wilting would not disappear in the late afternoons or during the nights but would become a permanent thing. If this happened, the trees' twigs and limbs would dry out. The trees might die. There would be leaf loss, and loss of the new spring fruit.

"Oh, for crying in a bucket," said Hazel. "Well,

what do the big grove owners do when their trees wilt?"

"They irrigate," said Felder.

"Then that's what we'll do."

"Will we?"

"Sure. Won't we?"

"No. Not their way anyhow. They can afford pumps and sprinkler pipes and all that. We can't, so we'll do it my way if it doesn't rain soon. You'd better pray for rain because you won't like my way. It'll be hard work."

"I don't care," said Hazel, saying precisely what she felt. To the right and to the left of the road the meadows stretched brown and dry, and just ahead was her brother's house. Its front yard was barren neat. Its backyard swimming pool sparkled blue-green.

Vannie Lee was up and dressed and yes, Hazel and Felder were welcome to ride into town with her, but she intended to be home again by one o'clock. Would they be finished with their business by that time, so they could ride back with her?

"Sure, sure," said Hazel, itching and twitching. "Can we go now?"

Said Vannie Lee, "You're in a hurry? I've never seen you in one before."

"It's different now," said Hazel.

"What's different?"

"Everything. I can't tell you about it. It's scary, and you wouldn't know what I was talking about. You want Felder and me to wait out here on the patio for you?"

Vannie Lee was not to be hurried. There was no hurry. Wouldn't Felder like to see the inside of her house?

Felder said that he would, and he and Hazel went in and followed Vannie Lee from room to shining room to gaze upon high-glossed furniture, groupings of wall plates, needle art, do-it-by-number paintings, and ceramics, ceramics everywhere. There was a collection of little silver spoons, another of glass bells, and yet another of china thimbles, all arranged either behind or under glass. Vannie Lee was so light, so sure, so prideful.

Happy as a dead pig in the sun with all this fool stuff, thought Hazel, watching her brother's wife bend to bury her painted face in a mass of artificial flowers. "Silk," said Vannie Lee, "and very expensive. Aren't they gorgeous?"

"Very," answered Felder. In the car on the way into Echo Spring he sat on the rear seat of Vannie Lee's car with his backpack laid across his knees.

At Vannie Lee's prodding, he admired the car's upholstery, its purr, the air conditioning and tinted windows, yet he sat as if caged.

Vannie Lee said that after her dance lesson she was going to go on to her ceramics class and Hazel grunted and with a searching stare turned sideways to observe roadside weed patches, acres of common earth, a water-starved lake ringed by sunburnt grasses. Maybe it would never rain again. This year God might forget to send any.

The thought of God, with whom she communicated as sparingly as possible only during those moments of required reverent silence just before classes started each school day, struck a fast, shapeless note within her—one note—and slid away. She jerked the thought of God around and set it in its usual nowhere corner. The car continued to eat the miles.

Saying she would be back for them around twelve-thirty, Vannie Lee let Hazel and Felder off in front of Mr. Bartlett's gate. Through the spaces between its high wooden slats, they could see the old man pottering around among his plants. There was no arrangement to these. Under shade and in the open, they were of many kinds and were everywhere. Vines that snaked along the ground and others that climbed. Dottings of freakish growths, some with dagger spikes and others with octopus arms. Star-shaped blossoms nestled in waxy green. Vagrant bushes. An army of sproutings in rusting cans. In back of all of this stood fruit trees, fat, healthy, sassy. Between the trees and the gardens lay a bog, a wet spongy area populated by masses of plant residue.

On the whole of this chaos Felder looked and looked, and after a moment Hazel said, "The bell's inside the gate. Pull the chain there and it'll ring, and then he'll come."

The bell pealed and Mr. Bartlett came to the gate, applying an eye to one of its gaps. At once his face lighted, yet in a tone of sly complaint he said, "Oh, it's you. I thought I was rid of you for the summer, but here you are back again to pester me. Why aren't you home thinking about money?"

"Now, now," said Hazel. "Why do you always act like you're not glad to see me when you are? You know I'm the only kid in Echo Spring you can stand. Let me in. I need to talk to you."

"Who is that with you?"

"His name is Felder Poole and he's my new partner. We're in business together. He's living in my grove house now. His mother and sisters too. He's going to fix my grove so all of it will grow again. When I sell it, I'm going to give him ten percent of what I get for it, that's how we're in business together. Come on. Open up this gate and let us in. We've got something we need to see you about."

Still with his face pressed against the opening in the gate, Mr. Bartlett trained an eye on Felder. "Young fellow, you're lucky."

"Yes, sir," said Felder. "I know I am."

"Our mutual friend here is a walking idea factory when it comes to business. It's a raw talent, I think. By that I mean I think it's one of those little quirks that come with certain people when they're born. Are you new?"

"Not very," said Felder. "I'm twelve."

"I meant new to Echo Spring."

Said Felder, "In that way I'm new. We only came here yesterday."

Mr. Bartlett made a wistful comment. "Twelve. I can remember when I was that age. That's when I found out I wasn't like other people and decided I didn't care. No, I'm wrong. I was only six when that happened. I remember I was just six because one of my front teeth was loose, and I asked my mother why and she said it happened to all little kids. I yanked the tooth out myself and that night put it under my pillow, and the next morning when I looked it was gone, but in its place there was a dime, just as my mother said there would be. What did you do with the first tooth you lost?"

"I kept it in a can of water for a week," answered Felder. "I thought it would grow, but it didn't, so I threw it out."

"I know a young lady who had the brilliant idea of renting hers," said Mr. Bartlett. "The good fairy who came after it left a dollar but forgot to pick up the tooth, so pretty soon every kid in her first-grade class heard opportunity banging on their doors and even paid in advance to get a whack at it. But as soon as they found out that the old fairy wasn't in the pay-now-and-settle-later business, they all ganged up on the tooth renter, and when they got through with her she came running down here, squalling her head off. It took me fifteen minutes to get the truth out of her, and even then I wasn't so sure I was hearing it."

"Not a one of them had a lick of sense and they still don't," said Hazel, arguing her own brand of logic. "They should have known the tooth fairy would look to see if they had any missing teeth of their own. And something else. I did not come running down here squalling my head off. I walked.

And you put some ice on me to stop the blood and keep the lumps from swelling up more, and then you took me home and told my mother I shouldn't roller skate in front of your house anymore because the sidewalk's got cracks in it and it's dangerous, and my mother said I didn't have any roller skates and I told her I had borrowed Jimmy Kitchen's. It was a story I made up, but it didn't hurt anybody. I don't know why you keep telling people about my tooth all the time. It isn't funny. Look here, you going to keep us standing out here all day?"

Mr. Bartlett's face disappeared. On the opposite side of the gate there was the click of a key being turned in a lock and the rattling of chain. The gate swung open and Hazel and Felder entered their host's world. It and he claimed Felder's entire thralled attention. He trotted after Mr. Bartlett's lean legs, bare to the knees, as though they might be a pair of stilted magnets.

"I keep telling myself that one of these days I'm going to put price tags on a lot of what you see here and sell it off for whatever I can get," said Mr. Bartlett, "but I can't stand the thought of opening my gate to strangers."

"What we came to talk to you about is bud sticks,"

wheezed Hazel, panting after her old friend and her young employee. "You got any extra ones you could lend us?"

Mr. Bartlett had a magnifying glass in his right hand and bent to gaze at a sprawling plant with a red, cone-shaped head. Straightening, he said, "Lend you? No, I can't lend you any bud sticks, but I'll give you some. Come. Let's go this way. What's wrong?" he asked, pausing to look back, for at a signal from Felder, both Felder and Hazel had braked to a stop. They were abreast of the bog now, and though Hazel had looked upon its plants before and had had their fiendish appetites explained to her, she had only listened with half an ear and had only looked at them from a wary distance. She did not for a moment believe that they were able to trap and eat bugs, and had never spoken of them to anyone except during that one off-guard jabber session with Wanda Poole.

Innocently shining in the sun, the wet-appearing plants were not beyond Felder's belief. At the sight of them, his eyes grew still and large. "Sundews. How long have they been here?"

Mr. Bartlett blinked and blinked again and looked at Felder as if listening to some pleasing and inner echo. "Years. They're perennial, you know. The older ones give up after about three years, but new ones always come. You want a closer look? Go ahead. Here. Take my magnifying glass and take Miss Iron Jaw along with you too. It might do her good to find out that there's more to what's here than she's thought about. I'll meet you in the grove."

"Listen," objected Hazel with some fervence, "we can come back and look at these plants later. Right now the important thing is the bud sticks, and we're wasting time."

"You certainly are," agreed Mr. Bartlett, "but I don't think Felder is."

Whistling, he set off down the pathway, and Felder, gentle with her unwillingness, reached for Hazel's hand and drew her to the rim of the bog, there to crouch, there to watch the nearest of the plants enact an eerie drama with a fly.

The plant was in flower, and beneath its long-stemmed white blossom, its rosette leaves, thrusting up from its roots, showed little hairy glands which oozed drops of clear, gummy fluid. Stuck fast to one of the plant's sticky leaves and entrapped in its juices, the struggling insect appeared to be exhausted and near death.

"Look," said Felder making use of the magnifying

glass. "Look. Do you see what's going on here?"

She saw. With knuckles pressed against her mouth she saw, first with horror and then with wonderment. The plant was a monster, lazy as all outdoors but clever, just standing there growing, standing there waiting for its food to come by so it could eat. People weren't that smart. They had to go out and earn the money for their food and go to the market for it and after that take it home and cook it.

Hazel leaned and with a finger touched the sundew's blossom and again, as in her grove the day before, there passed through her a sense of turning and finding. On the way to the grove, she ran ahead of Felder, liking the smell of heated earth, liking the droning and whizzing of flying things, liking everything.

Mr. Bartlett walked among his trees, caring not that they numbered less than a hundred. Careful volunteer hands had stripped them of the last of their late-maturing fruit and hauled it away to the county hospital, a delicious present to the old and the sick and the destitute. And now the pampered trees, sporting new, green fruit, stood waiting for the next go-round.

Hard and clean, the trees were Mr. Bartlett's children, and what good children they were too, not a coward or a shirker among them. Never whined about their food the way some human kids did, never yelled when they had to be sprayed for insects and diseases, didn't complain of the taste of city water during drought, didn't fall over in a faint the minute a little cold air hit the Ridge.

"It wasn't a little cold air that hurt my trees," said Hazel. "It was a whole big bunch. Even our house got cold inside. It got so cold I couldn't think, and when I got up the next morning I couldn't remember where I had put my left sock."

"Your left sock," said Mr. Bartlett.

"Yes. And you were out here all that time taking care of your trees. That's what you told me. Firing up your heaters and getting your wind machines going. I didn't even know my trees were mine then, but even if they had been, I couldn't have saved those that got froze because I don't have any grove heaters, and I couldn't have put any wind on them because I don't have any wind machines."

"That's tough beans," said Mr. Bartlett, "and I'm really sorry for you, but as soon as you get your grove all fixed up sweet again, somebody will come along and hand you your price for it, and then all your worries will take off like a spotted ape. Meantime let's get on with the bud sticks job if we're going to do it. They should be wrapped and labeled as we take them from the trees. I suppose you came prepared for that?"

"Felder brought everything," said Hazel, exultant. The bundling and wrapping of the bud sticks, each equipped with from five to nine buds not yet starting into growth, was handed to her, and it was an easy task, but there was also the labeling to be done, and in this she failed. Her hand wrote, but what it wrote she could not read, nor could Mr. Bartlett or Felder. Out of her failure she flushed what she thought to be a cunning explanation. "It's because I never heard of all these different kind of oranges, and I couldn't understand what you were saying when you called them out to me, so I had to guess how to spell their names."

Cruelly Felder judged one of the labels. "When I was four I could write my letters better than this. What does this one say? Parson Brown? Satsuma? Valencia? Hamlin? Murcotte? What?"

Faking, Hazel glanced at the label. "It says Parson Brown," she said, and waited for Felder to either agree or disagree. He did neither. The face of noon was yellow, and Mr. Bartlett offered a consoling pat and a potluck lunch. His kitchen was big and old-fashioned and the food he fished from his refrigerator was cold and heavy and good.

Life was good. Maybe a little on the shifty side because it didn't stand still, was always flopping around with new ideas and it didn't say exactly what they were all about either. But it was good. Good.

In her grove that afternoon, in a flood of comfortable obedience, Hazel worked with Felder long and faithfully. All thorns, branches, and twigs above and below the point in the rootstocks where the buds were to be inserted were removed. Then with his sharp knife, Felder made a downward cut about one and a half inches long, followed by a cross cut. When lifted with the knife, the corners of the intersection formed a little shield, a new home for the waiting bud. After that, using the plastic strips, came the wrapping and tying with the budding tapes, which would hold the buds snug and safe, in close contact with their new parents.

So went this work until the last of it was done and Felder, satisfied at least for the present, closed his backpack and announced his intention to call it quits for the day. Anxiously he spoke again of the leaf wilt in the trees in Hazel's grove. Except for the slanting rays that told of the coming sundown, the sky was void.

That evening Hazel and her father ate a lap supper on the Ryes' front porch. Her father said, "I saw your brother in town today, but he didn't have much time to give me. All he talked about was the boat he's fixing to buy. I'm real proud of that boy. Real proud. What about you? You got a few personal words for your old buddy? What'd you do today?"

"Felder and I went to town with Vannie Lee," answered Hazel. "Mr. Bartlett gave us some bud sticks from his trees, and then we came on back and worked in my grove. In one of my trees we put five different kinds of buds so when it grows up it will have five different kinds of oranges. It was Felder's idea. Have you ever seen that?"

"No," answered Millard Rye, and looked out across the unshaven lawn.

"It's just got to rain pretty soon," commented Hazel.

Her father set his empty plate on the porch floor. "It don't got to do nothing. I thought I told you last night I didn't want you getting too thick with that boy and his bunch."

"I haven't got too thick with them," protested Hazel. "Mrs. Poole and Wanda and Jewel went to town early this morning, and so it was just Felder and me and all we did was what I told you. Mr. Bartlett has got some plants that eat flies. Felder and I watched one. I was kind of sorry for the fly."

"I hate flies," responded Millard Rye. "They don't belong to live with people, and if I knew what jackleg it was what put them here, I'd call him up and give him a piece of my mind. I got a new order for you."

"Sir?"

"A new order," said Millard Rye with a touch of pepper in his voice. "I don't want you working out there in your grove anymore with Felder. You hired him to do the job for you, so you let him do it."

Stunned, unprepared, Hazel sat back and waited for her usual rescuers: rage, screams of argument, tears.

They did not come. This time there would have been no protection or power in them. In her father's puffed face and in the hard glint in his eyes, she saw that this was so, saw that he intended to win even if his winning might mean another of her hated silent treatments.

It was a moment of tension. Hazel was the first to give in to it. "Well," she said, "I don't mind that order if that's all there is to it."

"That's all there is to it," said her father.

"You told me to remind you to fix your chair," said Hazel. "You ought to do that before it gets much later."

Millard Rye rose and went into the house and returned with a hammer and a sackful of small nails. With loving whacks he repaired his chair and sat in it, contentedly rocking, rocking.

With its voices and waves of blurred odors, night was coming.

It was an old story this one: Hazel sprawled on the porch steps, her father in his chair, the conversation trifling. It was the same story, but now it was not whole. Its old solidness was missing, its threads were broken and swinging loose. Long ago everything in it had been discovered.

The evening odors were sweet, and Hazel sat inhaling them. There were lights in the Pooles' grove home.

"I reckon that woman and her daughters made it back from town all right," remarked Millard Rye. "I wonder did they get themselves the jobs they went after. But it's not any of our business if they did or didn't, is it?"

"No," said Hazel.

Said her father, "This is the way I like it. Just

you and me. Everything nice and easy. We don't need anybody else or anything else neither, do we?"

"No," said Hazel.

"Of course, it's nice when your mama is here too. I didn't mean it wasn't."

"I know what you meant," said Hazel.

"I think I'll go in and watch some TV. What about you?"

"Pretty soon," said Hazel.

"You're not mad at me, are you?"

"Oh, no," answered Hazel, guarding her altered self, holding it close.

5

The news that both Jo and Wanda Poole had landed jobs as maids at the Baptist Retirement Home in Echo Spring was brought to Hazel by the youngest member of the Poole family, who came with a bounce to the Ryes' back door. She carried a book and when she was asked to enter she did so on tiptoe. Following Hazel through the house to the leisure room, she had a fond nod for one of Millard Rye's favorite pieces, a wall picture of a careening bull with what appeared to be smoke billowing from his nostrils. Hazel had always thought the animal had about as much personality as a pasteboard box.

To Jewel Poole life was a hunt, a peering into all of its complexities. Hers was no morning of humdrum. Today she was a child of intention. "I'm supposed to find out where you are."

"If your eyes aren't stuck in your head on pins," said Hazel, "you can see I'm here."

"Felder wants to know if you're coming out today. I'm supposed to go back and tell him yes or no, but I don't have to hurry either way. Mama and Wanda went to work. They're going to clean for the good lady at the Baptist place where old people live."

Hazel lay on the sofa with one leg slung over its curved back. "You can go back and tell Felder I have to stay here till I can figure something out."

"Why?"

"Because my dad told me I had to."

"Are you sick?"

"No."

"Did you do something bad?"

"No."

"Then why?"

"I already told you once. My dad told me I had to."

"Is he mean?"

"No. He's good. But sometimes he doesn't like the things I do, so then I have to figure out what to do about him."

"Is that what you're doing now?"

"Yes. Be quiet. I'm thinking."

"About what?"

"About painting this floor in here."

"What color?"

"I can't decide. Maybe light black with some dark-black stripes."

"You think your daddy would like that?"

"No. He'd scream."

"I think it would look terrible."

"So do I," said Hazel and to comfort the death of this idea, found a weak laugh. The house was cool, too cool yet for the air conditioning. The windows were open, and beyond them there was the glittering day. From her position on the sofa Hazel gazed at the day and felt its pull, felt its gusto and possibility calling to her from some deep root. She thought of her mother in Tennessee who looked upon the telephone as an instrument of torture. Its voice was a troublemaker: a wrong number, somebody wanting a donation, somebody selling something, a decision to be made, a problem to be solved.

On the hassock beside the telephone stand sat Jewel, plain as a pebble and interested in all. "This is a nice house."

"Yes, it's nice," agreed Hazel.

"Have you always lived in it?"

"Always."

"All the houses we ever lived in made noise. Does this one?"

"No. My dad built it."

"Where's your mama?"

"Gone to Tennessee."

"When is she coming back?"

"I don't know. As soon as she gets tired of Tennessee, I guess."

"Why didn't you go with her?"

"Because I have to stay here and take care of my dad."

"Aren't you lonesome for your mama?"

"Sure."

Said Jewel, "When I'm lonesome I read one of my books." She opened the volume in her lap. "The one I'm reading now is about earthworms. I think they're wonderful, don't you?"

Ignorant of the marvel of all worms, Hazel explored the inside of her mouth with her tongue. "I never thought about them much, but probably if it wasn't for them, nobody would ever catch any fish."

"Fish," said Jewel. "Is that what you think about when you think about worms? Fish?"

"Fish," said Hazel. "Just fish."

Jewel clasped and unclasped her stubby hands. "Worms," she lectured, "make everything in the ground grow better. They work in the dirt and put air in it. All the dirt in the world has been through worms at some time or other. Through their stomachs. They're some of our best friends, but hardly anybody knows it. People know about dogs being their friends, but they don't know about worms."

"I had a dog one time," said Hazel and for Ticket, her once-upon-a-time little vagrant all wrapped up in curly brown fur, she experienced a pang. With Ticket she had shared her food and her pillow, and with her he had shared his fleas, his play rag, his ball, and his affection for yard holes. Ticket had lived on high wind and anything that could be dragged, shook, or yapped at.

With all of her trustful being, Hazel had loved

Ticket as she had never loved anyone or thing. To the neglect of almost everything and everyone, she had fastened her life to his. It took her a long time to get over his disappearance. For a week of days she had refused to accept it, had run up and down the road and then down to the creek and then into the grove and the forest back of the grove, calling, calling.

Only Vannie Lee had been of real help in her search, and when at last her father had called a halt to it, something in the way he held her hands, looking at them and not at her, had caused her to quietly and knowingly draw away, to heave a last shuddering breath for Ticket.

She had pretended. Ticket was gone and nobody knew where. She had loved him, but he had not loved her, the sneaky, two-faced little flea trap. Here today and gone tomorrow, that was the way of dogs.

Her pretense had saved her. After a while she was able again to be free and honest with her father. Her belief in his goodness and her love for him returned. In the evenings she again shared the porch with him and listened no more for a bark or a yap coming from the grove.

The grove. She needed to be out in it helping Felder, and here she lay like some miserable old cow waiting for somebody or something to put an idea in her head so she could get on with her business.

The empty eye of the television set caught her own eye, and she swung her feet to the floor and sat up. A little window in her head appeared, and behind its pane shone a face bubbling with suggestion.

"Ahhhh. There you are," Hazel said, smiling her delight and relief. "What took you so long?"

"What?" asked Jewel. "What is it? What do you see? Oh, did you get it figured out, and should I go back and tell Felder now? What should I say?"

"Say I'll see him tomorrow," answered Hazel and lay back nursing her enforced idleness. For her lunch she ate chili from a can and after that spent several hours hewing the story she intended to tell her father, providing its players with suitable backgrounds and believable names. Shunned, the television set stood in silence. The phone rang twice. She did not answer it.

At thirty minutes past four her father came from work. He was covered with carpenter's dust and said that his day had been one of the tackiest ever to come off the pike. He said he had a present for her and showed her a small tissue-wrapped box decorated with a puff of silver ribbon. "If I give it to you now, you won't open it till I come back from my shower, will you?"

"No, sir," said Hazel.

"It's something you been wanting for a long time," said her father.

She could not think of anything she had wanted for a long time, and when the moment came for the opening of the gift box, she had only a vapid stare for the two bright hoops nestled in jeweler's cotton. "Earrings," she said. "How pretty. And they're for me?"

Recovered from his tacky day and now in a mood of elation, her father fished one of the hoops from the box and dangled it in the light. "Fourteen-karat gold, and sure, they're for you. You don't think I'd spend as much as they cost me on anybody else do you?"

"But they're for pierced ears and mine aren't."

"Ho," chortled Millard Rye. "I changed my mind about that and I've arranged it too. Crowley Price is going to take care of that little old doodle-dee-do for you. He said for me to tell you to come on in as soon as you're ready to get it done."

"I wonder how much it will hurt," said Hazel.

"There isn't anything to it," crowed her father.

"You won't even feel it. The holes don't take but a minute to punch and then you'll wear some wires in the holes for a few days and then you'll be ready for your finery. You like them?"

"They're the most beautiful things I ever owned," said Hazel, and her father beamed his pleasure. His high good humor lasted throughout their bacon-and-egg supper, but by the time they had taken up their customary places on the front porch, his smile was tired and he lowered himself into his chair with a grunt. He asked about her day.

Hazel looked out into the lowering day. "It was finer than frog's hair."

"What say?"

"Finer than frog's hair. Fun. I wasn't bored a bit."

"I called you at noon. How come you didn't answer?"

"I was watching television. I guess I didn't hear the phone."

"I seen that kid Felder slinking around out there in your grove on my way in. Slower than pond water. Looks just like his mama. You notice that?"

"No," answered Hazel, "I haven't given his looks or any of the rest of him any consideration. He's my employee and that's all."

"I thought the reason you didn't answer the phone was because you were out there in the grove working with him," said Millard Rye.

"No sir," said Hazel. "I didn't go out of the house all day. I watched movies on television. One was about a little girl named Gloria. She didn't have any friends. She liked fires, and it showed her running around the town where she lived, setting people's houses on fire when it got dark, just so she could watch them throw their children out of the windows. The firemen only caught one. The rest all died. Horrible. Everybody screaming and crying. There wasn't any bad guy or any good guy. Just the little girl standing there watching. They didn't say she was a maniac or anything like that. They didn't tell what was wrong with her. They only showed half of it. Tomorrow they're going to show the other half. I don't want to miss it." The words came from her mouth in a pale, creamy stream.

Her father had removed the soft, loose slippers he wore around the house, but instead of dropping them beside his chair as he usually did, he sat holding them. He said that anybody who would run around setting fire to people's houses had to be missing some of his bolts. Beneath the calm surface in his eyes, there was a disturbance.

"I liked that movie," said Hazel, "and I liked the next one too. All about love. There was a boy and a girl in it. His name was Donald and hers was Darlene. They weren't married. I counted how many times they kissed. Thirty-five. With their mouths open. Like they were despert. Desperate. I didn't know boys kissed girls like that. Of course I only know about two boys. Jimmy Kitchen and Felder Poole, and they don't count. All Jimmy likes is those little hickey-jigger computer things he's always messing around with and his silly word puzzles, and all Felder likes is weeds and trees. Do you think it's going to rain pretty soon?"

"I can't say," replied her father. "It might. It might not."

"That least one of the Pooles, the one named Jewel, came to see me for a while this morning," said Hazel. "We talked about worms. She likes worms."

Said Millard Rye, "Does she? Well, I guess we've all got to have something to keep us from drying up. To my mind the Pooles are all a little bit on the daffy side. The boy likes weeds, and the little girl likes worms. I don't see any benefit in neither one, but if they do, that's all right with me. Weeds and worms never harmed anybody, I don't guess."

"No, sir," agreed Hazel. "Weeds and worms haven't got any harm in them."

"I don't want you watching any more TV programs like you watched today," said Millard Rye. "It's that kind of junk what makes criminals and trash out of children."

"Yes," said Hazel, "it does. It makes us have ideas." She thought she could hear worms at work beneath the floor of the porch, stealthily tunneling, eating dirt, filling their stomachs with it, putting air into it, expelling it, making it better for the world. Canny as a crow, she said, "I wish you'd let me get out there in my grove tomorrow and see what's going on. If I was out there to boss Felder, he'd move faster and get through with the job quicker. Like it is now, him and his bunch will be here forever."

"That is not a good prospect," said her father. And after a couple of minutes had ticked by he voiced a decision. "I reckon I'll let you off the hook. Tomorrow you can get on back out there if that's what you're so cracked on doing. Almost anything would be better than having you cram your head full of all that TV slop like you did today. But you watch yourself. I don't want to come home tomorrow evening and see you all played out. You do the bossing and let Felder do the work." He put his head back against the headrest of his chair. "Good grief a-mercy, I'm tired. I ought to go inside and phone your mama, but I'm just too tired."

"Rest yourself," sympathized Hazel. "We won't talk anymore now. You rest yourself."

She watched her father give in to his fatigue, and when he slept she went to sit on the floor beside his chair. The sight of his rough, limp hands caught at her, and she lifted the one nearest her and stroked it. A stinging force welled in her and she half leaned to her father. Sorry for her lies and sorry for him in a way beyond her understanding, wanting to give him something of herself, wanting him to know that she was truly his buddy and that she truly loved him and almost understood him, she nuzzled his shoulder with her chin.

6

At the brave hour of seven o'clock, Hazel returned to her grove the following morning. The air was sunlit, and she sucked her share of it into her lungs and sped through the trees, noting their curled leaves, curled from moisture duress, and that the areas beneath some of them had been cleaned of weeds and sod grass.

She found Felder at the rear of the grove house. He was kneeling beside several lengths of garden hose he had coupled, and was viewing them with a satisfied eye. Two metal laundry tubs and two metal buckets complete to ring handles sat in wait beside the hose.

Bright as the morning, Jewel was hopping around the yard, pretending to be a one-legged chicken. Felder's satisfaction was hers, and his plans were hers. She forgot to be shy. "Hazel," she called, "we're going to start watering the trees today. You going to help?"

"Yah," said Hazel and hunkered down beside Felder. Her blood was singing.

"But first," squawked Jewel, "we have to finish digging around the trees and get rid of the weeds so we can make little basins. We have to be careful when we do that."

"We'll be careful," said Hazel.

"The hose doesn't have any holes in it. It's not very long, but there aren't any rotten places in it. Felder found a jar of washers and put new ones in where it's hooked together. So it won't leak. He's smart. Don't you think he's smart?"

"Yah," said Hazel with tenderness shining, tenderness for Felder so pure and gifted, who furnished her mind that day with the taste of being linked to a system, to a life greater than her own. It had

Felder's language, which spoke of weeds and root and flower and stem as if it might be a sin to keep what he knew of these to himself, and yet the bigger, outer voice was there too. In the fading pink and the coming blue it was there, and to Hazel, the discovery of it was towering and muddled. More than once during the morning's toil she looked up, examining the sky, half expecting to see a pair of eyes gazing down at her.

Turned daytime white, the clouds strung out and then barely moved. Were they hiding something? Someone?

Under Felder's snappy-eyed leadership the work in the grove went forward, and was at once an agony and a conquest. First came the hoeing around those smaller trees that had not yet been relieved of weed and grass growing under them.

Hazel and Jewel made mistakes and Felder hurled corrections. "You're not after the trees, gnatbrains. What're you trying to do? Murder them? Didn't you hear me when I said you'd cut into their roots if you went in too deep? You're not after their roots. You're after the weeds and grass. So we can push the dirt around the roots and make cups. To hold the water. Don't chop. Set the blade of your hoe in like this and work it around like this so you can pull the weeds and grass out. So the ground will be loose. So it'll hold water. See? See?"

"We see," said Hazel and leaned on the handle of her hoe. She had put her best strength into her part of the hoeing. Her hair was wet to its roots with sweat, and she was black to her knees with dirt. In a little cool tantrum of rebellion she said, "We see and we hear too. We aren't deaf. You ought to be ashamed of yourself, Felder Poole, talking to your little sister like that. Calling her a gnatbrain. If that doesn't give you the guilts it ought to. Look, you've made her cry."

"I'm not crying," declared Jewel, dry eyed.

"Yes you are," said Hazel, "and it's nothing to be ashamed of. Whenever somebody talks ugly to me I cry. You need to blow your nose, honey? Here, use this leaf. I don't have any tissues with me."

Said Felder to Hazel, "Oh, stop. She's not crying any more than you are. I swear you positively perturb me. I wasn't talking ugly to you or to Jewel either. I was only trying to show you how to do this job right. Don't you want it done right?"

"I perturb your brother," said Hazel.

"He likes you," said Jewel without judgment, "and he only wants the job done right. He doesn't want us to murder the trees. He loves them, don't you?"

"Love them," breathed Hazel and was at peace again with Felder.

Out of sight but nearby, mourning doves grieved their contentment, and Felder returned to the grove house, making four trips to bring the tubs, the buckets, the hose swollen with water issuing from its deep well source. The hose had its limits, and so the tubs were filled and the buckets were dipped and carried to those smaller trees that had been basin ringed, each receiving several gallons of water.

Felder said that because of their size, to bucket water to the bigger trees would be like trying to quench their thirst with a teacup, and again he and Hazel clashed. She screamed her argument. "But they're as thirsty as the others! They need drinks too!"

Felder muttered and gave in.

So passed the morning, five hours of good endeavor. From time to time Jewel skipped off and came back proudly bearing a fistful of flowers, a stem, or a bit of vine, and Felder, ever watchful of her, took time out to squat in the brown-gray sand and give them names and explain their function. At the close of one of these work breaks he said to Hazel, "You didn't forget what I told you about the trees needing fertilizer, did you?"

Jolted, Hazel gaped at her partner. She had forgotten that she had promised to supply the money for fertilizer. She owned no money and owned no thought of a way to get any except to wait for her father's regular weekly donation, her allowance. As a saver of money she had always been a happy failure, in spite of her affection for its green and clank, but now here was this new condition and it was anything but a happy one. For money she had instinct, and it told her that her Friday two dollars and a half at a fertilizer store would scarcely buy her the attention of a clerk.

Scowling her humiliation, Hazel asked the necessary question. How much money was it going to take for the fertilizer?

Felder said he wasn't rightly sure. "We'll start out with whatever you can spare. I've decided we aren't going to do any spraying for insects. We haven't got the equipment and besides Mama said for me not to fool around with that. We've got citrus pests but usually they don't do much except ugly the fruit and trees some, so we'll let nature take care of them, but we'll need the fertilizer."

"Yes, yes," assented Hazel and hobbled home. After a vigorous shower and shampoo she lay on the sofa with her eyes closed, trying to think of where the money for the fertlizer was to come. After a while of this, her mind leaked an idea, and she rose, went to the phone, reached Donnie at his cab stand in Echo Spring and with him held an agreeable and productive conversation. Mr. Bartlett was next. With him Hazel also swapped a number of words.

Mr. Bartlett said he agreed with her that life was a hard job and why didn't she lighten her load and get out of the grove business? He said he knew a man who might take the whole mess off her hands for the right price.

"The price?" said Hazel. "The price? It doesn't have a price."

Mr. Bartlet said that he begged to differ with her, that everything had its price.

"Not my grove," said Hazel, and her next words fell on her ears as a shock. "No, sir. I'm not ever going to sell it."

Mr. Bartlett said he'd appreciate it if Hazel wouldn't scream in his ear. He said that not ever was a long time and idly inquired how many trees she thought she owned.

"Oh, I don't know," ranted Hazel. "Somebody said forty-eight to each acre, but the house takes up some of the room."

Mr. Bartlett wanted to know why her old, beat-up grove was of such consequence to her.

"Because that's where everything is," shrieked Hazel. "Don't you understand that?"

After a moment Mr. Bartlett said he believed that he did.

"People ought to think about that," pounded Hazel. "They ought to think about where the important things are, but they don't. All they think about is money, and it's a big, fat, greasy pain."

Mr. Bartlett said yeah, he thought so too. Said that money was nothing but a big, fat, greasy pain, and it would mightily please him if everybody would get away from the use of it, but he didn't see how that was possible. He wanted to know what Hazel thought her business partner would say when she told him she wasn't going to sell her grove. How, he wondered, was she going to square things off with Felder?

Reasoned Hazel, "Well, the Pooles are living in my house free and I'll figure out how to make up to Felder for the ten percent." Furtively she asked Mr. Bartlett if he knew how much fertilizer cost.

Mr. Bartlett said that he was not current on that subject, that the price of fertilizer went up and down all the time and that the man who delivered it to his trees always got the labor part and the fertilizer part mixed up, and to him it didn't matter which cost was which, because his trees and plants were all that kept him ticking. He said that he would be home all the next day and would be tickled to a peanut to see Hazel and Felder at his front gate at any hour they could manage. He said good-bye and hung up.

Hazel returned to the sofa and again lay with one leg hung over its back and her eyes closed, letting her idea ripen. At four o'clock the sound of her father's truck and then his light footfall announced his arrival. He carried a big, sturdy carton and a large, hardbound book and wanted to know how her day had gone. His shaggy face was kind and interested.

Bursting with her day, Hazel sat up. "Hee-yew. I sure found out a lot today. About things I never thought of before. When Felder tells about them, I feel like I've been in a hole all my life." Seeing the interest and kindness in her father's face begin to ebb, she leaped onto higher, safer ground. "I had sardines and crackers for my lunch. What are we going to cook for our supper?"

"Nothing," answered Millard Rye. "I brought it from town and it's already cooked and waiting for us in the kitchen, but it'll keep till I show you what I got here." He had lowered the carton to the floor and set the book beside it. Beaming his eagerness, he snapped his fingers at Hazel and said, "Hey, where's your curiosity? You haven't run out of it, have you? If you have, you can go on back and find it and bring it over here. What's in this carton is something you haven't ever seen or heard of before, sure enough."

Hazel went first to the closed carton, which told her nothing, and then to the book. The lettering on the book's cover looked up at her and she said, "A dictionary. Something like the one at school."

"It's to look up words we don't know," informed Millard Rye.

"Words about what?" asked Hazel.

"About this," answered her father. He had the carton open. His hands went in, wads of shipper's padding were cast out, and presently the carved hull of a ship's model, a sheaf of printed directions, and three large sheets of drawn plans occupied the space on the floor between the sofa and the television set. There were also a number of smaller boxes, an assortment of tools, and a cradle which had been lined with soft cloth and mounted on a board. Into the cradle went the hull.

Hazel's father gloated. "We are going to build us a little model boat like one of those what used to plow around out in the ocean. No, I shouldn't call it a boat. It's a ship. Ship people don't like it when you call a ship a boat. They get mad. The man I got this from used to be in the Navy. He was a lieutenant. I was at his house today doing him a repair job, and him and his wife was cleaning out their attic, and they came down and asked me would I be interested in this. Mrs. Lieutenant said they started building it several years back but got tired of it. She threw the dictionary in for free. Said she thought we'd need it. So now we got us a project like nobody else around here has got. Should we get started on it now, or should we go to the kitchen and pig up a little first? If all you had for your lunch was crackers and sardines, maybe we ought to pig up first."

Supper was a quick and modest affair, cold barbecued chicken and macaroni salad eaten from paper plates with throwaway forks, and then it was back to the model ship's hull and the mysteries of the sheets and drawings. The air conditioning purred.

Millard Rye was happy. Behind his smile there was strength and purpose, and his manner said that he intended to infect Hazel with both. Said he, "Now you see we got everything here to work with, and what I'm going to do first is give the deck of this hull another coat of shellac to seal in the grain. Mr. and Mrs. Lieutenant didn't get that far. While I'm doing that, you can start reading them directions. Do it out loud so I can hear it and so we can both be getting ourselves ready for the fun. I had me a little paint brush here someplace. Oh, here it is. Roo-dee-doo. Roo-dee-doo. Read, lady. Read."

Glad for him, and loyally glad that she was a part of his gladness, Hazel confidently lifted the sheaf of directions but after a moment of scrutiny confidence drained. The black words leered at her, their letters all running together in dizzying combinations. Hoping for relief, she flipped from page one to page two to page three searching for simplicity.

There was none. She took a gallant stand. "It says here, of all the painted something, the bottom finish offers the greatest something for something and is in the something of art."

"You're cheating," said her father, busy with his brush and can of shellac. "Don't give me all those somethings. Read it like it's wrote, elsewise we're going to get all mixed up before we even get started good. Go back and read now, and this time do it right. Read."

"I don't think this part has much to do with building the boat," hedged Hazel. "I think it's just telling a little story part. See? It's up here at the top. It's not with the rest of it. Look."

Millard Rye sighed. He leaned to look. Silently his lips moved. He drew back and resumed the task of applying shellac to the ship's deck. "You're right. That part hasn't got anything to do with how to put this thing together. It's a little story. Go on down the page a ways. Read."

"Down here," said Hazel, "it says you should put a reeve between the yard and the dead eyes." She had skipped through the words, interpreting them to suit her own vocabulary and said, "I didn't know a ship had a yard."

"I didn't either," confessed her father. "But if they say so, all we can do is take their word for it."

"I wonder," said Hazel, "whose dead eyes they're talking about and why they want us to put a reeve between them and the yard. What's a reeve?"

"Hold on," said Millard Rye. "I'll look it up in our dictionary. Let's see now. How you spell it?"

"R-e-e-v-e," said Hazel.

"R-e-e-v-e. R-e-e-v-e. Here we are. Well, sir. Aha. A reeve is a sheriff."

"They want us to put a sheriff on our boat?" asked Hazel. "Between the yard and the dead eyes? I think that's peculiar. Don't you think that's peculiar?"

"Yes," answered her father. "A little."

"I wonder where we're supposed to get the sheriff. How big is he supposed to be?"

"I don't know. Right now I'm not studying him."

"Maybe they want us to make one, but out of what I wonder."

Millard Rye had become irritated with the issue. He said that he didn't write the dictionary and he wasn't the one who had said there should be a sheriff on their model ship. "Tomorrow while I'm gone to work, suppose you study up on those directions so in the evening when I come home we can get right to work on what we're supposed to do next. For the time being, forget the sheriff. We'll find out about him when we get to him."

The bad taste of the difficult tomorrow entered Hazel's mouth. "Tomorrow I was going to town to get my ears pierced so I can wear my new earrings. Donnie already said he'd come after me about nine o'clock. That's the time he always goes now. He'll bring me home too."

Her father's irritation dropped away. His look was fond and indulgent. "You and them earrings. I thought you'd forgot about them. Naw, tomorrow you go ahead on to town with Donnie when he goes and get your ears taken care of. You can tell Mr. Price at the jewelry store I said charge whatever it costs to me." He was pleased, and when Felder came, he put on a mild show of welcome. "Come in, lad, come in. Nobody's going to bite you. Come in and see what my buddy and me have got here. You know what this is?"

Properly polite and properly interested, Felder advanced and stood looking down. "It looks like the beginning of a boat."

"Not a boat, lad," crowed Millard Rye. "Not a boat. A ship."

Said Felder, "It looks like it's going to be a lot

of work. I don't know anything about ships."

Hazel's father was looking into what the small boxes contained. "Yessirree, this is going to be a lot of work, but a lot of fun too. It's going to take my buddy and me all summer to get it done."

Offered Hazel, "We're going to put a sheriff on it. That's what the directions say to do. They don't call him a sheriff. They say he's a reeve."

"A reeve," said Felder. "I don't know that word."

Millard Rye left off with his examination of what the boxes contained and looked up. His curly mouth was handsome. "My boy, brighten up. There are probably lots of words you don't know, but that isn't anything for you to look so woe about. It's natural for somebody your age."

Leery of the purpose of Felder's visit, afraid that he had come to ask about the fertilizer money, Hazel bounded forward, flapping the sheaf of instructions. "The sheriff is supposed to go between the yard and the dead eyes. Here, you read about it."

Felder accepted the sheets. He read and delivered aloud what he had read. "This tells about the way of reeving lanyard between deadeyes. It doesn't say anything about a sheriff or a yard or dead eyes. I don't know what reeving is, or lanyard or deadeyes either, but reeving has to mean something you do. It can't mean a sheriff."

Hazel's father lifted the dictionary from the floor and handed it up to Felder. "It's old, but words don't change."

"A reeve is a sheriff," stated Hazel.

"Let him read it for himself," said her father.

Felder removed himself and the dictionary to a low table. On his knees before it, he studied for several minutes. He came back to Hazel and her father and announced his findings. "A lanyard is a piece of rope or a line of some kind that is used on ships to fasten something. It's passed through deadeyes. A deadeye is a rounded block made of wood that has either a rope or an iron band around it that's been pierced with holes so that the lanyard can be threaded through them."

"What about the sheriff?" asked Millard Rye with speculation and something else in his eyes.

"There's no sheriff," said Felder, standing his ground. "I think you must have read only one meaning when you looked up reeve. There's a whole paragraph about what reeves are and what reeving means. These directions talk about reeving, and when you do that, you pass a rope or something like that through a hole or opening in a block. That's what they mean for you to do. I didn't think reeving could mean a sheriff because reeving is something you do and a sheriff isn't. He's a person." With patience and wariness Felder closed the dictionary and set it on the floor. His mouth opened and closed. He swallowed.

Millard Rye was cleaning his shellacking brush. Without lifting his head he said it was getting on toward his bedtime.

Said Felder, "Mine too."

"Then good night!" cried Hazel, and in her rush to get to the door to usher Felder out, almost fell over her own feet. Returning to her father, to sit beside him, to view the model ship's glistening deck, she said. "It's going to be beautiful."

"Naturally," said Millard Rye without cheer, without anything. He gave the lid of the can containing the shellac a hard smack with the palm of his hand. "But let's stop now and telephone your mama. She might like to hear how we're keeping ourselves out of trouble, and we ought to remind her she's still got a home here."

Ona Rye was reminded. Her response was vague. She said she was not ready yet to come home and didn't know when she would be. She had found a Tennessee doctor who understood her headaches and her nerves and he was treating her for both. She hoped that Hazel and Millard were taking care of each other and would be able to work peaceably together on the model ship. She sent her love to all.

Upon the Rye household there then fell a rest. In the darkened house Hazel and her father slept in their separate rooms in their unmade beds.

7

The mayor of Echo Spring was one of those stormy, worthy women who not only never missed a working day but not much else of what went on in her town. From her second-story office she could look down and across a park and see the elaborate display of gold and silver and crystal in the window of Price's jewelry store, a sight which always brought a wrinkle of distaste to her nose, for she believed that the simple and natural things in life were the most vital and there was nothing simple or natural or vital in all that stylish brilliance.

The mayor believed in the freedom of resourcefulness, and in one of the morning hours of this working day was treated to the opening scene of what would soon become some resourcefulness, though at the time its promise was nowhere in sight.

At this early-morning hour it was the mayor's right to idle for a few minutes, and looking down into the street, she observed Donnie Rye's taxicab swing to the curb in front of Price's jewelry store. Chained to its rear bumper was a small hauling cart. From the cab three passengers alighted, the cab pulled away, and after a little sidewalk conflab, the girl who appeared to be in charge left her companions and with squared shoulders entered Price's store alone.

The mayor blew a sigh and turned back to the documents on her desk while in Crowley Price's plush store Hazel sat on a stool and had numbing ice applied to her earlobes.

Along Center Street the merchandisers were about their business. There was light traffic. The sun shone. A foot patrolman strolled his regular beat. A young secretary ran up the steps to city hall.

In her office the mayor signed three more official papers, left her desk, and again went to her window just in time to see Hazel Rye come from Price's jewelry store and join her waiting companions. The mayor had a glum thought and voiced it to her assistant. "Be it ever so daily."

"What?" said the assistant.

"Life in this town is just too daily," complained the mayor, and with good effect kicked the wastebasket, an act that did not make the front-page news in the afternoon edition of the *Echo Spring Ledger.*

Hazel and her two cohorts would not have agreed with their mayor. They were on their way to manufacture what they hoped would become a big and fruitful event, so there was no time for boredom. Having hashed and rehashed its details and its necessity to the point of exhaustion, there was now no talk of it as they left Center Street and cut through vacant sandlots, taking a short route to the avenue dominated by Mr. Bartlett's grounds and fifty-year-old home.

Meditative and observant, Jewel again reassured Hazel that she would not pester Mr. Bartlett, that she would only speak to him when he spoke to her. She said she understood how it could be that Hazel was the only kid in Echo Spring Mr. Bartlett could stand. She wanted to know how it felt to have ears pierced.

"Purely horrible," said Hazel, dramatizing the truth. "That sucker Mr. Price nearly killed my ears with his puncher-jigger."

She repeated this plaint to Mr. Bartlett, who offered her a moment of sympathy, obligingly inspected the thin temporary wires in her earlobes, acknowledged Jewel's presence, and wanted to know for what purpose Donnie had left the hauling cart at his gate.

Hazel and Felder took turns explaining, pleading their cause. Gravely Mr. Bartlett listened. Gravely he nodded his head or shook it, but in the end said he thought their idea might be a sound one. He would, he said, pay Felder and Hazel twenty-five percent of all monies received from the sale of those of his plants that were either surplus or unwanted.

So the gate was opened to the cart, which was drawn around to the rear of Mr. Bartlett's house and placed on the clean floor of his open-air potting shed.

There was great industry. Jewel did not take a part in this. Holding her interest in check and holding herself aloof, she sat with the books she had brought along, solemnly turning their pages.

From Mr. Bartlett's cluttered garage there came paint brushes, a hammer, a saw, a jar of nails, a sheet of plywood, and buckets of paint. Mr. Bartlett left the shed for a few minutes. When he came back, he carried a length of sheer candy-striped material and with a flourish showed it to Jewel. "I can't think why I bought this. Possibly because it reminded me of my wife. When I go to the cemetery to put flowers on her grave, I always take red and white ones. Isn't this pretty? I think it will sew up nicely. Which do you think would look better on our cart here? Ruffles all around the roof it's going to have, or some tieback curtains at each post?"

With careful ardor Jewel said, "I think ruffles all around the roof would be so cute. Like a little petticoat."

First Mr. Bartlett knelt and then he sat, bending his kind attention. "Do you always read two books at the same time?"

The question went unanswered for several minutes, for Hazel had left the work on the cart and plunked herself down in front of Mr. Bartlett. There were specks of red paint on her shirtfront and in her hair and on her bare arms, and there was elation in her face. Three sides of the cart's body were now a gleaming cavalier red. "It's going to be gorgeous," said Hazel. "Gorgeous, gorgeous."

Mr. Bartlett turned and studied Felder, who was still painting, and studied the cart. He whistled through his teeth and said the cart was certainly beginning to look as if it might have a future, but his interest returned to Jewel and her books. He was gentle and serious. "You didn't answer my question. Do you always read two books at the same time?"

"Sometimes," said Jewel, "I get in a hurry and read three. My dad did that and so does my mother, so the rest of us do it too. They taught us."

"Was your dad a teacher?"

"No. Mama said he should have been one, but he liked to work where things grow. We have always lived where things grow."

Inquired Mr. Bartlett, "Where is your dad now?"

There was a glow in Jewel's delicate smile. She placed a finger across her lips and with another pointed to the sky.

Mr. Bartlett reached to take up one of Jewel's books from her lap. "This looks like something I might choose. I like the bird on its cover. Is it about birds?"

Jewel's soap-and-water face shone. "One. His first

name is Fred and his second name is Ted and he can talk and lives with a doctor. The doctor keeps him in a cage and when little children come and have to have shots Fred Ted helps. He runs up to the door to his cage and says, 'This won't hurt a bit.' And then the children laugh and forget to be scared."

"Fred Ted sounds to me like he more than earns his birdseed," commented Mr. Bartlett.

With a palm Jewel smoothed her clean smooth skirt. "Yes. Last year my teacher had me stand up and read the whole book to my class. I couldn't do it all in one day. I forget how many it took."

Ignored, forgotten, Hazel sat stiffly watching and listening. To her teacher she was fascinating, but never had she been asked to stand and read a whole book to her class. And never had Mr. Bartlett looked at her as he was looking at Jewel now. As if she might be one of his plants or trees. Smart kid. Always with her nose stuck in a book. Smart little squeak, always so clean.

Hazel swallowed annoyance and exerted herself. "In my class Jimmy Kitchen is always the one who has to stand up and read, but I won't have to listen to him when I go back to school again. I'm rid of him. Forever. Ha!"

On Hazel, Jewel turned a questioning gaze, and as though he might be telling the time of day Mr. Bartlett explained. "Our mutual friend here didn't pass her grade last school term so she's been retained. She'll be in sixth grade again next school year."

At once Jewel was all sympathy. "Retained. That's awful. I'm sorry, so sorry."

Hazel swallowed yet another bigger dose of annoyance. "Thunder. Retained is nothing. Don't you feel sorry for me. I don't need anybody to feel sorry for me. I get along. You know why? Because I have ideas all the time. Hairy ones. They're so hairy they scare me. They don't come out of books either. They're mine."

Mr. Bartlett had restored the story of Fred Ted to Jewel's lap and had taken up her second volume, opening it to its first leaf. Behind the panes of his spectacles his eyes grew wistful. "Rivers of the world. Now here's a subject big enough to make anybody rear up on his hind legs and beg for more. The Orinoco and the Amazon. I always wanted to see those two, and might get around to it yet if I can keep on breathing long enough."

"Those rivers are in South America," said Jewel. "If I ever get to go look at any of the big ones, I want to see the North American ones first. Like the Columbia."

Like a river itself this discussion went on and on, and tingling with a shrewish kind of discontent, Hazel left it and returned to Felder and the cart. Presently Mr. Bartlett left Jewel to her books and sauntered over to kneel and draw chalk lines on the sheet of plywood, to engineer the problem of designing a flat roof. It was decided that it and the cart's wheel spokes and four corner posts would be painted white. "But not today," directed Mr. Bartlett. "Tomorrow." He stood and rubbed his knees and flexed his shoulders. Felder dipped his brush into red paint and applied it to the cart's tongue.

Across town the noon train whistled its arrival and departure, and Donnie rang Mr. Bartlett's gate bell, shouted "Lunch!" and sped away. At two hours past noon he was back to collect his three nonpaying passengers. On his head his cap was jaunty and on one of his ring fingers a gaudy stone flashed its gem colors. He sang all the way to the Ryes' front gate. Felder and Jewel did not loiter. Felder said each of them had work waiting for them at home.

In the Rye kitchen Hazel stood looking at its accumulation of household soil, and in her father's room and then her own she stood looking at the rumpled beds and the strewn clothing. She went to her closet and looked in, fretfully noting a lifetime of collections, bits and pieces of things she had hoarded with the someday intention of turning them to some use. Junk, all of it, and it smelled of dust and rot.

Peering into the closet's darkest corner, she spied two of her hated books, and recognizing the first as one of those Jimmy Kitchen had read aloud to her sixth-grade class, dragged it out. The light in the room was good, and she sat on the floor with her back against a chair leg. The book in her hands was not heavy, yet when she opened it, its monstrous wording assailed her. Faster and faster she flipped the pages. Tears of mortification filled her eyes. When the last page had been turned, she closed the book and for a time remained where she was. Her tears were gone. Her head was high. A vault in her mind had opened.

It was later than usual, nearly seven o'clock, when her father came home. Full of swagger he entered his kingdom by way of the back door and stopped short, blinking and sniffing. He saw that his kitchen table had been cleared and was set for two. A runner of paper toweling decorated its center. The sink was empty, as was the garbage box. There were the mingled odors of household cleaning agents, chlorined scouring powders and pine-scented detergents.

On a stool next to the refrigerator Hazel sat tensely waiting. From skin out and from top to bottom she was viciously clean. She watched her father walk to the stove and set two delicatessen boxes on its cleared top. He identified their contents. "Our supper. After I wash up we'll eat and then we can get right to work on our ship." He turned to fully survey the room. "You had them Poole women in here again to clean?"

"No, sir," replied Hazel. "I did it and did your room and mine too." Her hair was still wet from its shampooing and she leaned forward to better exhibit her ears. "I had my ears pierced today."

"I'm proud to hear that," said her father. He had turned back to the stove to open one of the boxes, dipping into it with a thumb and forefinger to lift a dark meat gob to his mouth.

"We live like pigs," said Hazel.

Her father swung around and his smile came delayed. "When did you decide that?"

"I didn't decide it. It's true. We live like pigs."

"If you didn't decide it, then how come you're thinking it?"

"I'm thinking it, that's all."

Millard Rye's expression did not change. "Well, that's interesting if it isn't anything else. What else are you thinking before we get off the subject?"

"I am thinking," said Hazel, "about my brain. What Mr. Bartlett said about it. And what he said about Jimmy Kitchen's. I told you about it and all you did was laugh."

"Because it was funny. What's wrong with laughing when you think something is funny? Looky here, what's this all about? Here I come home from beating myself to a frazzle all day and find my good old comfortable house all stunk up like a hospital and my buddy sitting in a corner looking at me like I just crawled off a snake farm. Girl, what ails you?"

Hazel fixed a relentless eye on her father. "Why didn't you tell me what Mr. Bartlett meant when he said my brain was worth ten thousand dollars and Jimmy Kitchen's was only worth a hundred? You knew, and it was your place to tell me, only you didn't and I've been made a fool of. What are you doing?"

"I'm going to eat while I'm still able to swallow," said Millard Rye, bringing the opened delicatessen box to the table. He sat, eased his feet from their heavy work shoes, and picked up his fork.

"Jewel Poole knows how to read as good as Jimmy Kitchen, and she's only eight years old," said Hazel.

"There's nobody holding you back on learning how to read as good as Jimmy Kitchen," said her father. "I pay for you to go to school. They got teachers. It's not my fault you don't know tat from bat."

Hazel flung a direct challenge. "It's your fault I'm like you are. You want me to be like you. You don't care when I play sick and stay home from school. You don't want me to know tat from bat, because if I found out, then I'd know more than you."

Her father threw his fork at the stove, pushed his chair back and the word fight was on, maintaining its heat for the better part of half an hour. At its end, Hazel slung her boxed supper out the back door. Her father strode through the house and sat in his front porch chair, wrathfully rocking, while in her room Hazel prowled, looking for something to smash.

She passed her full-length wall mirror and was shocked by her image. Her face was stark-white and her eyes were wild. A perilous thought flooded her mind. Trembling, she opened the door to her closet, and from one of its shelves took down the only piece of luggage she owned. Her father would shrink a foot when he looked in her room the next morning and found out that she had run away. He'd shake and roar and dance around like a chicken with its head chopped off, but by that time it would be too late for him to say he was sorry. By that time she would be long gone. She wouldn't go to Echo Spring. She would take the road that went the other way and wouldn't do any traveling in the daytime. In the daytime she would sleep in the woods or somebody's orange grove, and do her traveling by night. For money she would sell her earrings. In the next town she would go to a jewelry store and do that, and then go to the train station or the bus station and buy a ticket. To where? And what would she do when she got there? Thunder. Where and what didn't matter right now. She would figure out the answers to those questions later. Later.

Her suitcase was packed and ready to go. She

closed its lid and snapped its locks into place. At the windows there was that half-light that is neither honestly night nor honestly day.

Waiting for the full night to come and waiting for her father to go to his room so that she could leave without fear of being caught, Hazel stored the suitcase in her closet and lay on her bed with her arms upflung on her pillow. The windows in her room faced west and she watched the sky change its drifting colors. What made them, and where did they go when the next-day ones came again?

Watching the mystery of this, Hazel was seized with a sense of smallness and nothingness. She rolled her head from side to side and thought of Mr. Bartlett and the Pooles. If she ran away, the Pooles would go, her father would see to that. And Mr. Bartlett would wonder. He would hurt.

With a heart full of trouble, Hazel put a fist to her mouth and pressed. And thought, if I run away there won't be anybody to talk to Sir, nobody to help him build his ship, nobody to sit on the porch with him or watch television with him. The others don't really care anything about him. Mama's always sick with her headaches and nerves, and all Donnie and Vannie Lee think about is buying stuff for themselves. They don't ever want to go to Bernie's and eat steak with Sir or go to the movies with him. They're always too busy for that.

An hour later Millard Rye passed Hazel's open door. Her lamp was on, the suitcase in her closet had been emptied, she was clad in a pair of clean pajamas and was sitting spraddle-legged in the center of her bed. There was an open book in her lap, and without looking up from it, she said, "It's pretty awful between you and me sometimes, isn't it?"

"Pretty awful," answered her father. "But when it's good, it's good." He was bathed and ready for his bed and said, "Good night, lady."

"Good night to you, sir," responded Hazel and put her book aside. Her windows were black, and when she switched off the light on her bedside stand, the room went black.

In the darkness, in the stillness, Hazel lay back, suffering. "Uhhhh," she said. "Uhhhh."

8

The mayor of Echo Spring had had the advantages of a good education, and for this the male rulers of the town were grateful. They were not so grateful that Her Honor was also the product of a country childhood, which had left her with more barnyard sense than could be gracefully handled at times. She conducted the duties of her office as laid down by the edicts of the town, yet she had days when officialdom seemed less important than humandom. Today was one of those.

At her desk the mayor finished her second cup of morning coffee, consulted her appointment calendar, held a brief conversation with the chief of police and moved on to the next subject. Her assistant came teetering in with the mail, placed it where it belonged and crossed to the windows.

"Anything happening out there?" inquired the mayor.

"I think so," replied the assistant, "but I'm not sure what it is."

The mayor got up and moved to the windows. What she saw made her forget that her hair was gray and that at the end of some of her workdays she was ashamed of life.

Being drawn and pushed by one boy and two girls, a small hauling cart was being placed in the center of the park that lay across the street from city hall. Each of the children wore a head kerchief matching the ruffle sported by the cart's flat roof, which was graced by dwarf palms standing in plastic containers. The cart itself was a festival. Even to its wheels it glistened, red and white. Its cargo of varied potted plants was a rich display.

The mayor opened one of her windows. "They're setting up shop."

"The air conditioning is on," said the disinterested assistant, "and aren't you wasting it? You're letting the cold air out and the hot air in."

"You've got a couple of problems," said the mayor. "Number one is you've got no imagination and number two is every once in a while you turn into an adding machine. Don't I have a pair of binoculars around here someplace? Find them for me."

The assistant located the binoculars, and holding them, the mayor knelt at the open window. "Yep, that's what they're doing. They're setting up shop. They're going to sell their plants. I wonder what that silverware tray is supposed to be for? Oh, that must be their cash register. Look. There comes their first customer."

Fretted the assistant, "I wonder if they have to have a peddler's license? Shouldn't they have a peddler's license? They're on city property."

"Fudge," said the mayor. "You're license happy just like everybody else in city hall. Why is it we must all have licenses for everything these days? Call up the *Ledger* and get hold of Mr. Doflunky or whatever his name is and tell him I said if he wants a picture and a story about America to put in his newspaper, to send a reporter and a photographer down there. Do I have time to go down there myself and find out how much those kids want for their palms?"

"No," answered the assistant, while in the park Hazel dealt with First Customer, a lady who was attracted to the cart's begonia section, but who wound up buying a fern and a pot of Swedish ivy. "Ivy is so talkative," she commented. "And it's easy to propagate."

"You're right," purred Hazel. "I propagate every one of mine every day, and they lap it up." Flushed with the success of her first sale, she poured on the charm, hovering first over her pad-and-pencil additions and then the money tray, which Mr. Bartlett had stocked with small coin-and-currency change.

The charm was lost on First Customer. She peered at the change Hazel deposited in her palm, counted it twice, and said, "You're a good little saleslady, dear."

Already a celebration, Hazel's day took on an even greater height. "Because I like being nice to people."

"But you've given me back too much change," said First Customer and returned sixty-five cents to the tray.

When she had gone, Felder left off fussing with the cart's plant arrangements, came around to check on Hazel's pad-and-pencil figures, shook his head and ambled over to one of the park's trash depositories. From it he fished a folded newspaper, searched through its sheets, came back to the cart with one sheet and borrowed the cashier's pencil. He sat in the grass beside Jewel, and as fast as he could write, began filling in the little squares on his newspaper sheet. Among the grasses and in the bushes and in the full-leafed boughs, there was insect commotion and warmth and growth, and Jewel, wide eyed as a grassflower, watched the street. She wanted to know where all the customers were. "If we had a whistle and blew it, then they'd know we were here," she said.

For Felder, Hazel had a question. "What are you doing?"

Felder was secure. "Working a crossword puzzle."

"A crossword puzzle. Jimmy Kitchen is always doing those."

"Good for Jimmy Kitchen."

"Are they hard to do?"

"Some are. Some aren't."

Struck by the aloof pity in his tone, Hazel said, "It was only sixty-five cents, Felder, and she gave it back to me."

"Did I say anything about that?"

"No, but you're thinking it."

"Propagate," said Felder resting his pencil.

"Propagate? Is that one of the words in your puzzle?"

"No, but it's in one of yours."

"How is it in one of mine? Which one?"

"The one you told that lady about. You don't know what propagate means, do you?"

"I might have heard of it before."

"You might not have too. It means to multiply. It means to multiply, and you do it with seeds or roots or shoots or cuttings. And you don't do it every day, not to the same plants. From now on," said Felder, "I'll be the cashier." He turned back to his puzzle, and in an instant of despair and lost patience, Hazel went around the flower cart twice, and the despair in her rose to a penetrating pitch. She watched Crowley Price come from his jewelry store. He was accompanied by his clerk, and both stood at the edge of the park, gawking and pointing.

"Yes," bellowed Hazel, "it's true. Come on over for a good look if you don't believe it."

They believed it. So also did the reporter and the photographer from the *Echo Spring Ledger.* The photographer leaped around, snapping pictures from all angles, and the reporter said, "Marvelous. Makes me homesick."

"For what?" asked Hazel.

The reporter scratched his head. "I don't know. Probably for something I never had."

"We need customers," said Hazel. "So far we've only had one."

"The customers will be here," said the reporter. "We'll pass the word along on our way back to the office, and they'll come."

They came. Singly and in pairs and trios the shoppers came. Captivated, they bought until only three plants in the cart remained and interest in these was being observed only by a lone latecomer. This was a young man who might have weighed around a hundred and thirty pounds and might have measured close to six feet. He had a smooth, open face and the smile of a choirboy, so when he sidled up to the unattended money tray and began transferring its coins and currency to his pockets there was shock and disbelief among the cart's owners.

Jewel was the first to recover. She threw up her arms and delivered a scream which affected the thief not at all. Still smiling, he said, "Don't do that again, kid. Don't any of you do anything or say anything unless you want some real trouble."

Felder reached for Jewel and tried thrusting her behind him but didn't succeed. She was not merely angry, she was mad. She darted forward, charging the thief full tilt, and he swung around and struck a blow to her head that felled her.

"Hey!" cried Felder. "Hey, you!" and ran toward the thief and jumped on his back. The thief could not shake him, could not rid himself of the legs clamped around his middle or the hands which pulled his head backward.

Astonished and seeing her own chance as an avenger getting away, Hazel rushed to the cart, pulled a plant from its can, took quick aim, and let fly. The thief received the full brunt of it. The plant landed on his nose, and its loose, damp soil flew up and out in all directions.

Still trying to rid himself of Felder, the thief began to stagger around. There were gobs of dirt in his hair and in his eyes, and he moaned, "Oh, I can't see. You've blinded me."

"Police!" roared Hazel. "Police! Somebody!"

The sight of Jewel's white, terrified face infuriated her, and without thought for herself she lunged toward the thief, who tried to kick her. He missed, and she charged in and sunk her teeth into one of his forearms. "Police! We're being robbed! Police! Hang on, Felder! Don't let him get away!"

"He's not going to get away," gasped Felder. "He's got our fertilizer money. Grab on to his belt in the back and hang on, but watch out for his feet."

Swiping another bit of time from her desk duties, the mayor was again at her window, binoculars in hand, and seeing all that was taking place in the park, ordered her assistant to call for a policeman.

Response to the call was fast. In a matter of minutes a peace officer stood by the cart in the park, trying to sort some sense from the situation. He looked at Felder, still clinging to the thief's back, and looked at Hazel, still holding on to the thief's belt, and said, "Somebody had better tell me what this is all about."

"It's about me coming in here and trying to buy a plant for my mother from these crazy kids," said the thief, spitting dirt, clawing it from his hair and his eyes. "Everybody else was buying from them, so I didn't think there was any danger to it, but quick as all the others left, the kids jumped me. They tried to rob me."

"What," inquired the policeman of Felder, "are you doing on this man's back?"

"I'm protecting our property," asserted Felder. "He's got some of our money in his pockets, and he hit my little sister."

"I'm blinded," wailed the thief. "It was the biggest girl there who did it. She threw a plant and all this dirt on me. Bit me too. Lookit here. See where I've been bit? Lookit my arm. You better get me to the hospital emergency room quick, and you better find out who these kids are. They can't go around attacking innocent citizens like they did me. I'm going to sue their mamas and daddies. I know my rights."

Purple with rage, Hazel let go of the thief's belt and ran around to stand in front of him. "You dumb liar catbird. I ought to shoot you twice! You weren't trying to buy a plant for your mother or any such thing. You were stealing our money, that's what you were doing, and we want it back. Give it back now!"

Looking undecided, the policeman had taken hold of the thief's arm. "Fella, I don't think I've seen you around Echo Spring before. Suppose you show me some identification."

"My eyes is my most precious possession, and now they're ruint," groaned the thief. "Ruint. I can't see a thing. Get this kid off my back, will you? And don't let the one who bit me come near me. Where is she?"

"She's right here," said the peace officer and issued an order. "You kids back off. Go sit someplace and stay put till I can get this straightened out." There was a shout from across the street, and he pivoted and located its source.

The mayor was at her open window and was yelling. "Officer, wait a minute! Wait just a minute! What kind of a story is that young man feeding you?"

"I haven't got the whole of it yet," shouted the policeman. "But he says he's hurt and needs to go to the hospital. He says he can't see. He says the kids jumped him and tried to rob him while he was trying to buy a plant for his mother."

"Aside from his eyes, ask him how badly he's hurt," squawked the mayor.

Said the policeman to the thief, "The mayor wants to know how badly you're hurt aside from your eyes."

The thief turned and looked across the park to the mayor's window. "That's the mayor? You got a woman mayor?"

The policeman tightened his hold on his prisoner and sent his answer back to the mayor. "He's not hurt too bad. Got a little dirt in his eyes and one of the kids bit him and that's about it. But I'll take him on over to the hospital and get him checked out. He might need a shot for the bite."

The mayor had won her part in the case without half trying. "You do that! You have him checked out good at the hospital, and then you take him on over to the jail and tell your boss I said give him a bed in a quiet cell. He's going to need all the rest he can get. Before I get through with him, he might wish for the permanent kind. Oh, and one thing more. Have pretty boy there empty his pockets and give those children back their money, and never mind if he claims not all of it is theirs. I'll take full responsibility if there's any question about that. Tell your boss man I'll see him in about thirty minutes and will give him my official report on this whole matter." With more force than was necessary, Her Honor closed her window, and in the park Hazel, Felder, and Jewel restored themselves and their business to order.

Jewel had an ugly welt on her forehead, and for the treatment of this, Hazel went begging. Crowley Price went to his cold-drink refrigerator and handed over some ice wrapped in a small towel. He said he was sorry both he and his clerk had missed out on the show. "We're trying to take inventory today, and I guess we were in the back room all the time it was going on," he said.

"It wasn't a show," said Hazel and trotted back to the park.

With the ice pack on her welt, Jewel lay in the grass, and Felder sat beside her working his crossword puzzle. He had tallied the money in the money tray and found its total to be correct. Far off, the kind of clouds that bring rain gathered, and Felder sat poring over his words, writing, writing.

Feeling herself adrift, Hazel lifted the plant which had served as her weapon against the thief. She observed its broken spine, its denuded roots and wilting leaves. Sorrow for its lost life licked at her, and she crawled around on her knees, using her hands to scoop up the black dirt which had been the plant's home, dumping it back into the pot which had contained it.

On a husky note the wind whispered, and Hazel looked up. The sky was immense, and after a long look at it, Hazel turned back to the dirt in the pot, creating a hole in its soil with two fingers. Into the hole went the battered plant. Its stem refused to stand erect, but its roots would dig down and spread, and soon there would be new life in the pot.

Certain of herself now, certain of everything, Hazel bent to the plant and in a lowered, secret tone spoke to it. "Grow," she said. "You grow, you hear?" Her head was in a whirl, and within her, something sizzled.

9

Hours before the rain came, the plant cart, covered with sheets of clear, protective plastic, was back in Mr. Bartlett's potting shed, and along with two hefty bags of citrus fertilizer, Donnie had returned Hazel, Felder, and Jewel to the grove house on the Rye property.

Helping Felder lift the fertilizer from the taxicab's trunk and carry it to the shelter of the Poole's back porch, Donnie said a doctor had told him all about those good-deed people called Good Samaritans, and now he knew how it felt to be one. "But I don't mind telling you I'm glad to be done with this."

"Done with this?" said Hazel. "With helping us? You mean you aren't going to help us anymore?"

"Now listen," protested Donnie. "You got to look at my side of it too. I got one, same as you."

"Well, I will be mortally jiggered," said Hazel.

"You got your fertilizer," argued Donnie, "and that's all I promised I'd help you with."

"Two bags," said Hazel, "and they won't go twice around a gimlet. We need more, so we've got to go back tomorrow and make more money to buy it."

Jewel made an earnest report. "When we were in the park today, a man came and took our pictures and another one asked us our names and wrote down everything we said."

"Oh, hush about that," said Hazel. "That wasn't of any account, and we need to talk about this other now."

Donnie said he didn't know what a gimlet was, and Felder said he didn't either, but he guessed it might be something small.

With his tongue Donnie washed the flashy ring

on his left ring finger and said Hazel had no call to look at him like he was something that had just crept out from under a stump.

Hazel took a melancholy stand. "You're so stingy with your promises. You never stretch them. I'm your little sister and you never do anything for me unless I fall down on my knees and beg you."

Donnie's interest in his ring was finished. He put his hand in his pocket. "I don't remember any time you ever fell down on your knees and begged me for anything. Except the day Vannie Lee and me got married and you wanted to be the one to cut the wedding cake. You made a first-degree mess out of it too. Slopped it all over the preacher. I had to pay to have his suit cleaned."

Without a trace of conviction Hazel said, "Thunder. I was a pain then. Maybe I still am because nobody likes me. Nobody wants to do anything for me. I don't blame them. Nobody likes an ugly pain."

"You are not ugly and I never said you were a pain to me," declared Donnie, looking pained. "All I said was I was glad to be done with this. I didn't know I wasn't. Just tell me how many more days you reckon you're going to need my free gratis services, so we'll both know."

Again the captain of the game, Hazel said, "I can't say exactly. All I can say exactly is it won't be more than a few little ones."

Before he left, Donnie inspected Hazel's ears and said it looked to him like Crowley Price had done a good job piercing them.

"He said I should keep the holes clean and I'm doing it," said Hazel, and for the fifth time in her memory, Donnie kissed her.

The welt on Jewel's forehead was no longer. Where it had been, there was now only a faint blue streak. In the west the clouds continued to bank and darken, and Felder said he hoped they would bring water to the grove, but if that happened it would be better to wait with the job of fertilizing, because a heavy watering could bring a wash, and a wash would mean loss of the tree food. He said it was his turn to cook supper, and that for one thing, he thought he would make a cornbread.

In the five o'clock emptiness of her own home, Hazel set her precious pot of dirt and wilted plant in a pie tin, and after dousing it until it would drink no more, placed it in the center of the kitchen table. The pot's drainage holes leaked dark water, and now there was water at every pane.

The long-waited-for rain had come, and Millard

Rye only beat its first adventurous tempest to his door by inches. He was in a high-hearted mood. "Let her rain. It'll wash my truck, and you'll get to ride back to town with me in the kind of style as befits a lady of your station." He spied the plant on the table and said, "What's that?"

"A plant," answered Hazel. She was showered, shampooed, and dressed, ready for one of Bernie's Friday-night steaks. "I see you got yourself a haircut today," she remarked.

Mischievously her father put his thumbs in his ears and waggled his fingers. "Two," he said. "The first one looked so good I went back and got another one."

On the way into Echo Spring he talked of buying a car. "We ought to buy us a automobile. Your mama don't care nothing about one because she don't know how to drive and don't want to learn and never wants to go anyplace much anyway, but you and me ought to have us a automobile. This old hack is good enough for me to rattle around in. It's sort of my trademark, but a stylish lady like you deserves to have some stylish wheels under her whenever she rolls into town. What would you say to us buying ourselves a Cadillac?"

The rain was throwing crazy shadows on the road,

and Hazel leaned forward, watching them. "When would we go and pick it out?"

"Maybe come Sunday," answered Millard Rye.

"I didn't know they sold cars on Sunday," said Hazel.

"To a man wanting to sell a Cadillac, I don't imagine it being a Sunday would differ much," said her father. "What color you think we ought to shoot for?"

"Yellow," said Hazel snatching at the first color that came into her head. She was listening to the rain which was coming straight down, filling the hollows in the road. All this water, she thought. So good for my trees, so good for everything. The notion of spending Sunday buying a Cadillac struck her as being silly and useless. "But I don't know," she said. "If the man hasn't got a yellow one, a blue one or a purple one would be pretty."

Her father said he didn't think that the car people in Detroit or wherever it was Cadillacs were made put together purple ones, but come Sunday they would find out. He steered his truck around a large puddle and steered his conversation to another subject. "Before you got out of bed this morning, I was out in your grove looking around. Looks to me like you've been keeping that Poole boy busy. What's his name again?"

"It's Felder," said Hazel.

"Felder. That's right. I keep forgetting it. I guess because that is not a usual name. I'm not saying there is anything wrong with it. It's just not usual, is it?"

"No," responded Hazel, "it's not usual."

"And he's not usual," said Millard Rye. "Anybody can see that. He's the kind will always manage to get along. Has he said anything to you about when him and his outfit intend to move on?"

The air in the truck's cab was warm and moist, and the air in Hazel was not to be ordered. In her lungs it began to push and strain. "No, sir," she answered. "He hasn't said anything to me about that. It'll be quite a while yet I think. My grove looks a little better than it did, but there's still a whole bunch more stuff has to be done."

Her father said, "Well, I was only asking. It's your fish fry and looks to me like you're doing a good job bossing it."

Because of the rain there was an early false gloom, and along Echo Spring's main thoroughfares the streetlights were on. In front of Bernie's hole-in-the-wall steak house the parking spaces were all vacant.

Bernie said he didn't mind his lack of customers, because in wet weather his wife always got a backache and had to go home, leaving him to hold down the fort by himself.

Hazel and her father took their usual table, the one nearest the kitchen, and when Bernie brought their steaks out and set Hazel's down in front of her, he made his usual comment. "Don't stint yourself on the ketchup now. I got another bottle in the kitchen, and it's got your name on it." Her father always laughed at this, but she didn't see a thing funny in it. She liked Bernie's steaks, but his jokes were older than water.

Bernie was a gleaner of newspaper gossip. Nothing in the pages of the *Echo Spring Ledger* escaped his eye, and concerning what he read, he took vast pleasure in beating his customers to the punch. Secondhand, some of Bernie's reportings made little sense unless you let your mind drift with them, because Bernie was a fast talker and enjoyed adding fiction to fact.

On this night Bernie's item was firsthand, so it made sense. In offering it to Hazel's father, Bernie's style was droll. He laid the front page of the daily edition of the *Echo Spring Ledger* on the table occupied by Hazel and her father and stood back.

Millard Rye only glanced at the paper at his elbow. "What's that?"

"It's today's paper," said Bernie. "You mean you haven't seen it?"

"I don't read newspapers much," said Hazel's father. "Nothing but trouble in them. Has somebody robbed the city dump?"

Bernie drew a chair out and sat down opposite Millard Rye. "Millard, did you know we got us a hunk of real America right here in our little old town?"

"I have heard that a couple of times," said Hazel's father, "but I don't mind hearing it again. What's the story and who told it this time?"

"It comes in two parts," said Bernie. "The mayor had to tell the second part. There's quite a piece there about the whole thing. The picture is interesting too. Millard?"

"Bernie," said Millard Rye, "shut up. I am trying to find America in this picture here, but all I see is three kids mooning around some kind of a doo-dad loaded up with plants. Which is supposed to be the America part? The doo-dad or the kids?"

Hazel coughed, reached for her water glass, and

without stopping, emptied it. Her father turned his head to give her a look and returned to his study of the newspaper picture. Squinting, he bent to it, and in a minute his expression changed. "No. Somebody tell me no."

"Yes," said Bernie smiling happily. "It's true. But read the story, Millard. The story is the best part."

Hazel's father planted his gaze on Hazel. "I don't want to read the story. You tell me what it says and don't leave anything out."

"I haven't read it," objected Hazel.

"But you know what it's about, don't you?"

"Yes, sir."

"What's it about?"

"Felder and Jewel and me selling plants in the park. To make money to buy fertilizer for my grove."

"Whose plants? Where'd you get them?"

"From Mr. Bartlett."

"Did he give them to you?"

"We're friends. You remember that time I got beat up at school and he took me home?"

"Yes, I remember it," said Millard Rye. "But we was talking about the plants. Did Mr. Bartlett give them to you?"

"No. He only said he'd give us twenty-five percent of every one we sold for him. They're some he's got too many of and wants to get rid of. He helped us fix up that cart that belongs to the Pooles so it would look pretty and we took it to the park and sold all the plants but three."

"Who'd you sell them to?"

"Ladies."

"And that's what this story in this paper is about? You peddling plants to ladies?"

"No sir. That's not all of it. After we sold all the plants but three, a man came and tried to steal our money, and Jewel hollered and he socked her and that made Felder mad so he jumped on the man's back and I threw a plant at him and bit him. And then a policeman came. That dumb liar catbird robber said it was us trying to steal his money, but the mayor stuck her head out of her window and yelled that we were the ones telling the truth. So the policeman took the robber away and that's all."

"The catbird is in jail cooling his heels and probably having thoughts about swiping money from little kiddies," said Bernie. "What are you so heated up about, Millard? It's a great story. Everybody in town is laughing."

"I'm not laughing," said Hazel's father. He had

taken his wallet from his pocket and was counting out the money to cover the cost of the two steak dinners. They were only half eaten, and at the last minute Bernie deposited what was left of them in a bag and handed it and the newspaper to Hazel along with a consoling comment. "Your friends might like to see themselves in the paper."

The rain had stopped. The earlier false gloom was gone, and now in the true evening gloom it was just dark enough to clearly see the first star.

During the homeward ride, Hazel's father drove at his usual careful pace, grumbling a word or two to the rain-slicked road, while in her corner of the truck's cab Hazel huddled in silence, certain that her father was cooking up one of his explosions. The truck's windows were open, and in the meadows on both sides of the road every wild night thing croaked and hollered and carried on.

The silence stood out, stretched out, and when it became too much for her, Hazel exerted herself. "I don't know why you're mad at me. You told me if I needed money to fix up my grove, I'd have to go out and earn it, and that's all I was doing. I didn't know they were going to put my picture in the paper and write that story about me and Felder and Jewel."

"I am not mad at you about that picture and that story," declared Millard Rye. "Newspapers can't sell blank pieces of paper. They've got to put pictures and stories about people in their papers so they can sell them. That's how they make money. So I'm not blaming you there. What I'm blaming you for is, you're always tearing around every which way doing things without checking them out with me first. What if I had wanted you to go somewheres with me today? What if I had fell off somebody's roof and broke my neck and had some dying words to say to you? The doctor wouldn't have knowed where to look for you, now would he?"

"I was in the park," said Hazel. "Donnie knew where I was, and so did Mr. Bartlett. If you ever need me quick for anything, you call up Mr. Bartlett's house because that's where I'll be if I'm not at home. Or else I'll be in the park. Mr. Bartlett's got a lot more plants we're going to sell for him. Today," she said, "we made enough off what we sold to buy two bags of fertilizer for my trees. Mr. Bartlett is a sweet old plug and he likes me. I'm the only kid in Echo Spring he can stand. Isn't that something?"

The truck was ascending a rise, and Millard Rye waited until the road ahead lay flat again before giving his answer. "Yes, that's something, and I'm proud to hear it. But listen, lady, I'm afraid I've got to ask you to put an end to your business with Mr. Bartlett."

"Sir? What did you say?"

"The business of you selling plants for Mr. Bartlett. I can't have that no more. I can't have people thinking my lady has to get out and work so she can buy what she wants. That puts a bad light on me, don't you see?"

Hazel fell back against her seat. "You want me to tell Mr. Bartlett I can't sell any more plants for him? But it was my idea. It wasn't his. And now if I go and tell I can't do it anymore, what will he think?"

"You tell him what I said about it shedding a bad light on me, and he won't give it more than a minute of his thinking time," said Millard Rye. "He wasn't born yesterday morning."

Groping for some door of escape from this destruction, Hazel said, "We're friends, and when I told him about my idea for Felder and Jewel and me selling off the plants he had too many of, he was tickled silly." To hide her ugly tears she opened the bag containing the remains of Bernie's steaks, snatched a piece attached to a bone, raised it to her mouth, and began to gnaw on it. Her tears, she knew, were useless. Her friendship with Mr. Bartlett, she knew, was at an end. The plant sale in the park, her picture and the story about her in the newspaper had nothing to do with it. It was all her father, her father, with his meddling, jealous tricks that said one thing and meant another.

She was so sure of this that her father's next words came only as a confirmation. "I tell you what," said Millard Rye, "tomorrow I'll go by and have a little talk with Mr. Bartlett myself and explain how things are with us. That way you won't have to mess with it and he'll understand."

With the greatest difficulty Hazel said, "Tell him I said I'm sorry. And tell him Felder and Jewel might want to keep on selling his plants for him without me. If they don't, I'll ask Donnie to go after the cart and bring it on back here." This time she had no heart for battle and sat with her shoulders hunched and her fingers clamped around the gnawed steak bone.

"Being a daddy to a child like you is not an easy job," remarked Millard Rye, and when Hazel did not tackle this comment, he said, "Hey, look at our headlights. The left one looks cocked to me, don't it look cocked to you?"

"To me it looks the same as the right one," replied Hazel. "Straight."

"I guess my eyes must be failing me," said her father. "Lately I notice things look different to me than they did a year ago, especially when I go to read something. Reading gives you a screaming-meemie fit too, don't it?"

"Yes," said Hazel.

"Then come Sunday," joked her father, "when we go to get us our Cadillac, you watch me and I'll watch you. Between us we ought to be able to make sure I don't sign anything that's going to gyp us. We can't let that happen. Your old dad has to work hard for our money. I didn't mention that to make you feel guilty, you understand. I'm supposed to make the money we need, and speaking of that, when we get home I'm going to give you your regular week amount and give you the extra you'll need to buy the rest of the fertilizer for your grove too. We'll have Donnie bring it to you. Does that stick with you all right?"

"That sticks with me all right," said Hazel. And to avoid further conversation with her father, so lavish in his victory and so embarrassingly transparent, she poked her head out of the window as far as it would go and kept it there until her father brought his truck to a stop at the Ryes' front steps.

There was no work on the model ship that night. Hazel and her father went straight to the porch and sat in their accustomed places. There was a little talk of this and that. The night flowed. Frogs prophesied more rain. And after a while, in his chair, Hazel's father slept.

When she was sure that he was soundly so, Hazel rose and padded into the house. From the living room she took the dictionary, and from the kitchen she took her plant.

In her room she set both on the floor beside her bed, and thinking, thinking, she sat down beside them. A beetle banged against a window screen. Something within her darted and rolled, and as if glimpsing the answer to it, as if she might find it in the plant, she leaned to it. "Don't you die on me. Please don't die on me. I need you."

The room was still, still. The lamp on the bedside table cast its glow, and Hazel turned her attention from the plant to the dictionary. With steady fingers she laid it open and faced her world.

10

There was no more rain for a week, though the air remained humid, and every afternoon gray-blue cloud humps rode the northwestern rim of the horizon.

Now a yellow Cadillac stood parked in the Ryes' front driveway, and Hazel's gold earrings dangled from her earlobes.

The ship's model lay neglected on the living room floor. Whenever Hazel had one of her housecleaning streaks, she was careful to vacuum around its plan sheets, its hull still in its cradle, its bits and pieces. Millard Rye took no note of the absence of the dictionary. In the evenings he and Hazel took rides in the new car and afterward watched old Western movies on television or sat gabbing on the porch until Millard either fell asleep in his chair or went to his bed.

Hazel's bed partner was the dictionary. Furnishing her with an outlet for something she could not name, its maddening words fought her and she fought back. So many words, all so hard to copy, to learn. So many words, some with more than one meaning, and she was years late.

At night behind her locked door, working with her pencils, her writing pads, and the dictionary, there were times when she felt the full rumblings of self-doubt, and to muffle the sighs and groans brought on by these, she would bury her head in her pillow. But then she would think of her father and of Mr. Bartlett and Jimmy Kitchen and Felder and would grow quiet and be sure again. Confidingly, the words in the dictionary lured her, and there was passionate satisfaction in the thought that with the passing of each study hour her brain became cheaper and cheaper.

During these days it was Felder who led the work in the grove. He had his own hardheaded formula for smoothing things out and for pushing disappointment and change of direction out of the way. "We've got our fertilizer, and that's all I'm thinking about right now," he said. "Did you come out here to help us spread it, or are you just going to stand around bumping your gums all morning?"

"Tell me," said Hazel. "Tell me again what Mr. Bartlett said when you and Donnie went after the cart."

Felder continued his task of scooping fertilizer from bags into buckets. "He said your dad had been to see him."

"I don't mean that part. I mean the other."

"So then he wanted to know if just Jewel and I wanted to sell plants for him in the park, and I told him we'd do it later but not now. I told him first I had to stay out here and finish what I started. Then we loaded the cart with all those plants he wanted you to have, and the books to go along with them, and he said for me to tell you to be good to yourself."

In the distance the low-lying scrub meadows held the morning ground fog, and in Hazel there was a long ache. With slow emphasis and slower courage she said, "Felder, I have to tell you something."

"Where's Jewel?" asked Felder looking up from his scooping.

"I don't know. Gone back into the house for something. Listen. You'd better listen to me. I have to tell you I've decided not to sell my grove. I'm going to keep it for myself. I don't know for how long. Years I think." Her voice didn't sound like her usual one. It sounded as if all the breath had been squeezed from it. "So I don't know," she said, "how I'm going to pay you what I promised. Except you can still live in my house free for as long as you want. Felder?"

The expression in Felder's eyes was mellow. It offered nothing and everything. He hefted one filled bucket, testing its weight. "You didn't have to tell me that. I already knew it. Here. See if this bucket's too heavy for you. If it is, we'll dump some of the fertilizer out."

Hazel stood holding the bucket, which was too heavy. It pulled at the muscles in her shoulder. "It's not too heavy for me," she said. And asked, "How? How did you know I wasn't going to sell my grove?"

"I knew it," answered Felder, "that first day when we were out here starting the budding, and I knew it more the first time we went to Mr. Bartlett's and looked at the sundews."

Still holding the overweight bucket Hazel took a step forward and looked down at Felder, who was on his knees filling another bucket. She wanted to reach down and touch his hair or the back of his neck. The ache in her lengthened.

"I don't know how much I would have owed you if I hadn't changed my mind about selling my trees, but I'll figure it out, and I'll give you a dollar a week on it till I get it all paid. I'll be regular with it. You won't have to come after me for it. My dad gives me my allowance every Friday night, and I'll give you your dollar every Saturday morning."

Felder did not say whether he would or would not accept her weekly dollar. He gave Hazel a curious smile, and she smiled back. Jewel came from her house errand, Felder doled out the rules for the day and the work in the grove began.

Felder lived to create. He could not let the world be. That day the fertilizer was spread, bucket by bucket and tree by tree. And that day the wrappings from those rootstocks that had been budded were removed. Unions between the buds and the stocks had taken place. The buds were alive and healthy, and to coax them now into growth, Felder lopped the rootstocks and made cuts about three quarters of the way through the stocks on the same side as the buds and about two and a half inches above them. The lopped top parts of the stocks were then pushed over to lay on the ground, where they would continue to nourish the rootstocks so that chances for the survival of the buds would be increased.

"Now," said Felder, "as soon as the buds grow a couple of inches, all the stock tops should be cut off, and as soon as the buds grow some more, they should be tied and staked so they won't break off, and as soon as other buds and suckers come on from the rootstocks, they should be pared away." With the sleeve of his T-shirt he wiped fertilizer dust and grove dirt from his face. "What are you going to do with those plants Mr. Bartlett sent you?"

"I'm going to make a special place for them somewhere back in here where they'll be safe and nobody will bother them," answered Hazel. The sight of the buds so new and the sight of the repairing trees made her heart laugh. All was good, and the thought that she had made a part of it possible filled her mind.

That day she had to run. There were squirrels and jays in the grove, and she ran after them, imitating their chatterings and callings. And stopped and looked up, and in the high blue sheen she saw purity and energy. And promise. She could not rid herself of the feeling that a strong, kind promise was up there. It was watching her. It knew her and liked her. Her heart laughed again.

With Felder's help that day, Hazel selected a site for her precious plants, a spot close enough to the grove house so that water would not be a problem. The location would provide shade for the shade lovers and sun for the sun lovers.

During this activity Jewel crept after Felder. When she spoke to him it was in whispers. He put his arms around her and, listening, either nodded or shook his head.

This happened too often, and Hazel, roused to suspicion and several moments of vague anxiety asked, "Is something wrong? Does Jewel need something? Is she sick?"

Felder was brusque. "There's nothing wrong and no, Jewel isn't sick and doesn't need anything. She's just being a baby today." He put Jewel aside and went to the cart, which was standing now in the backyard shade of the grove house. "Come next winter when the weatherman hollers frost warnings, some of these little guys will have to be covered else the cold will get them."

The anxiety in Hazel slid away, "Yah, yah," she said and skipped home to sit in her room, poring over the illustrated plant books Mr. Bartlett had sent her. When her father came, he wanted a ride in the Cadillac and a steak at Bernie's. He wanted to sit on the porch and talk. "Bernie's sure got a way with steaks, hasn't he?"

"Yes," said Hazel. That strange, half yellow, half brown of Florida's Ridge dusk lay on the land. The lights in the grove house were on, and from her position on the porch steps Hazel could see the Pooles moving around in their rooms.

Millard Rye rocked. "Our new car just floats, don't she?"

"Yes, sir," agreed Hazel. "She just floats."

"Your mama ought to be coming home soon. You reckon her visit in Tennessee has changed her any?"

"It might have helped her some," said Hazel. "I hope so."

"Everybody ought to get out and make a change once in a while," remarked her father. "It's good for them, but most people are not bright enough to see it. Them that can't are just sitting around collecting dumb-dust."

"Yes, sir," said Hazel. "That's what they're doing."

"Come give your old dad a little smoochie and let me go on to bed," said Millard Rye. "I'm as tired as if I'd been ironing overalls all day."

Sometime during the night the Pooles pulled out. Hazel discovered that they had gone when she went to the grove house the next morning and saw her plants sitting in a neat arrangement on the back porch. In the center of them there stood a jar half filled with black seeds. The cart was gone and the house was newly cleaned. Only that which had belonged to the Pooles had been taken from it. Not one written word had been left for Hazel.

For a while she crouched beside her plants with her face in her arms. Her thoughts dodged in all directions, and they numbered in dozens, but when at last they rested, there was only one left. It nailed her father, and there was no guesswork in it. It was sure, like looking at money.

He did it, she thought. Sir did it. I don't know how and I'll never ask him how, but I know he did it. There was a glitter in her eyes, and she raised her head and centered her gaze on the jar of seeds, recognizing it, remembering that she had seen it first on the day she had cut into Felder's puffball.

In the terrible silence Hazel reached for the jar, holding it cupped in both hands. There was safety in the feel of it and a force in her surged upward.

From the grove there came the comic calling of an unseen, winged singer. "See what I see! See what I see?"

Hazel looked up and out. She took a grip on her voice and the jar and said, "Oh, don't be so smart mouthed. I see what you see. Naturally I do. I see more than you see." Her throat ached. There was an ache in her chest. "These seeds here for instance. You don't know why he left them for me but I do. He wants me to plant them so when I go to the park and he's there selling plants for Mr. Bartlett, he can ask me how they're doing and I'll say fine. They'll do fine. I'll make them do fine."

"See what I see!" sang the hidden caroler, but this time Hazel ignored its voice. She had the jar open and was carefully tilting it so that some of the seeds ran out into her palm. Their promise, the life that would come from them, was secret now and helpless, but this would not be for long. The seeds were real and what they meant was real. In the earth they would make roots and after that there would come their stems, their leaves and flowers, their beauty.

Down along the banks of the creek the grasses whispered, and upon the grove and out beyond it, the climbing sun rained down its dazzling light.

About the Authors

With the publication of their first book, ELLEN GRAE, in 1967, Vera and Bill Cleaver created a sensation in the world of children's books. Since then they have broken all the rules, combining daring contemporary themes with the traditional values of humor, imagination, authenticity, and fine writing, and they have received outstanding critical acclaim. "That children's books are richer for the Cleavers there is no doubt," said *The New York Times* on the publication of WHERE THE LILIES BLOOM.

Books by the Cleavers have been nominated four times for the distinguished National Book Award and have been included on such important lists as the American Library Association's "Notable Books," *The New York Times*'s "Outstanding Children's Books," and *School Library Journal*'s "Best Children's Books."

Vera Cleaver was born in South Dakota; Bill Cleaver in Seattle, Washington. Together they have collaborated on 16 books. *Hazel Rye* was conceived by Vera and Bill Cleaver and completed by Mrs. Cleaver after her husband's death.